The Next Door Neighbor

By: Danielle Walker

ISBN: 0991412427
ISBN-13: 978-0-9914124-2-6

YJLM Publishing House
www.yjlm13productions.com

Printed in the United States of America

ISBN: 0991412427

CONTENTS

Acknowledgments i

Living Single 1

Crazy man 15

Something's off 27

Lights out 39

Good morning 43

Snooping around 55

Rain on me 65

Cookies anyone 77

Scripper love 85

Thug Life 97

Life's a Witch 109

Trust no one 117

ACKNOWLEDGMENTS

I would like to first thank my lord and savior Jesus Christ, for allowing me to write my second book out of seven. If it wasn't for him this journey wouldn't be possible. And I pray he keep me through the next five and continue to keep readers intrigued by my imagination. I would like to dedicate this book to all of my Dreamers that have supported me from day one with book one 'The Ultimate Betrayal'. You guys have been awesome and I really appreciate the support. With patience, the next five will blow your mind.

LIVING SINGLE

The moon was rising as the presence of the sun was only a mere memory. A cool breeze dashed through the city as the clouds eased their way into the abyss. Brown and orange leaves danced on top of Cameron's window as she sped across the 285 and 85 conjunction bridge singing 'Cruise Control' by J-dro. The 'Lac Muzik' album was one of her all-time favorite albums to listen to whenever she was out and about. "Baby sit back cause I got it on cruise control... Da, da, da, da, da." She sang. As she rocked and swayed while weaving through traffic.

From the time she left home, till the moment she was currently indulged in. Her speed-o-meter had been playing paper, scissors, rock between 95mph and 105mph. Funny how the police are never around when speeders take to the road. Taking a sip of her green tea as she cut the driver off to her right, without using her turn signal. Cameron merged off the expressway and continued down Jonesboro rd. until she pulled into 'Lashay's' parking lot. Climbing out of her vehicle after turning the ignition off, she reached back in for her tea and slammed the door. Because the store closed at 12:00 a.m., she had to knock on the window for someone to let her in.

"Open the door!" She yelled and waved at the employee that passed

1

her with a broom in his hand.

"Ms. Stephanie!" He yelled. You got somebody standing at the door!" Staring the lady up and down as she waved and motioned for him to open the door. "Do you want me to let her in?"

"Let her in!" Stephanie instructed. "That's Cam!" Making her way to the front as she scribbled on her 'end of the shift' chart.

Meanwhile, the whole time Cameron was awaiting to get in. She had been looking around the parking lot to make sure no one crept up behind her. Jonesboro was quiet, but mama didn't raise no fool. Things could get a little risky after hours if you wasn't aware.

The guy finally unhooked the latch and informed her, she could come on in. Prancing through the lobby, Cameron placed her belongings in the first booth behind the trash bin closest to the exit. She took one last swig of her refreshing tea just before she tossed it in.

"Buurrrrpp." Holding her stomach as a massive belch burst out. "Excuse me," she chuckled.

"Just nasty!" Stephanie sang as she caught the culprit of the funky smell red handed.

"I said excuse me." Laughing as she followed the foot prints that were plastered on the floor which led to the front counter. "How was your day?" She asked as her eyes roamed the menu board. Eating ground beef wasn't one of Cameron's favorite dishes, but if it was free. She'd eat almost anything.

"Stressful like always, when I come in this hell hole." Singing as she wiped the cold from her eye.

"Why won't you apply somewhere else then? I know a couple places that's hiring right now. Especially for seasonal workers." She suggested. "With your managerial experience. You're bound to find something promising." Enthusiastic about the potential possibilities that are available for Stephanie.

"I've thought about it." Looking up at the ceiling as she contemplated on Cameron's voluntary suggestions. "But the schedule they've given me here, works well with Rico's schedule. And we both know I have to be free when he comes in town." Thinking of how strenuous it is already on her to make time for her boo. "That's the only time we have to spend with one another by him being gone for weeks at a time. All of the time." Pissed, because she didn't realize what she was getting herself into when she agreed to date a truck driver.

"With that being said, when I ask you from here on out about your day at work. I don't want to hear none of that complaining you be doing." She advised sassily while she rolled her eyes. "I'm just going to throw my hand up and you can talk to the hand, because at that point I ain't trying to hear nothing you got to say."

"If you say so." Rolling her eyes as she continued to scribble. "Since you feel it's alright for you to come in here and interrogate me about my life. And get frustrated with me because I didn't portray my feelings the way you thought I should. What's the word on yours?"

"Ain't nothing new over here or out the ordinary with me." She said as she leaned over the counter popping her tongue. "Oh, I take that back." Raising one finger in the air. "I saw a moving truck at my old neighbor's house this morning." Fumbling her keys in her hands.

"Did you get a chance to see who it was?" Stopping her pen halfway into the sentence she was writing.

"Some dude." Cameron stated nonchalantly as she waved her hand as if she was swatting at a fly.

"Did he have any kids?" Suddenly vested in the details of this new neighbor and his personal affairs. "Did you see any women?" Wondering if

3

she could eventually play match maker with him and Cam.

Cameron had been single for a couple years now and it thrilled Stephanie to attempt to stab cupids arrow in someone's butt for her. She didn't have a problem with getting any dates. Cameron was very attractive and guys asked her out all the time. But she would turn them down if they didn't meet her dating qualifications. Everyone had their own standards check list they'd create that an individual had to live up to. At least the top 5 from the list had to be on point, in order to get a phone call. She didn't consider it being shallow or picky. She just kept in mind she'd be the one that had to wake up next to the guy. Besides, Cameron had a few old faithful's she could dial when she needed a fix. One or two dedicated maintenance men that didn't mind clocking in when the furnace needed some attending to. Having that luxury was more than enough attention for her. She enjoyed not having to commit. Freedom was a bliss for her and she wanted to ride that wave for as long as she could.

"I don't think so." Taping her index finger on her cheek. "I didn't see any children's furniture or any women helping him that I can recall. I was too worried about rushing Bear to hurry up and use it so I could go." Trying to remember if she saw anything that could have suggested he had a family. "I think it's just him, but I won't know for sure until he gets settled."

"You're right." Nodding in agreement. "Is he cute at least?" Giving Cameron her undivided attention as she hung on by a thread awaiting her response.

"Yeah... He's alright." Wanting to change the subject because she had no interest in dealing with men outside of the ones she already had. "You should make him a cake and take it over to him." Deviously trying to figure out a plan on how to get them introduced.

"Are you out your rabbit ass mind!" Standing at attention. "I know what you're trying to do and you can forget it!" Grabbing one of the peppermints out of the plastic bowl that sat in between the cash registers.

"Don't cheat yourself, treat yourself." Stephanie encouraged while laughing. "You need a man, not a toy. And we both know he meets three of your qualifications guaranteed, already."

"And what's that?" Sucking on the hot peppermint.

"Well, he has his own place."

"Yes… But he's too close to my personal space."

"Has his own car." Using her pen to check off a mark on an invisible list in the sky.

"We don't know if it's his, his baby mamas, or his mothers."

"He's handsome."

"He may not even like women."

"And, he got money obviously because he stays in your neighborhood. That makes four."

"Seriously, I'm not about to entertain this mess. You need to finish what you got to do so we can go. I'm getting sleepy now."

Cameron lived a nice, cozy, quiet life. She worked her nine till five and drove one of the most expensive luxury cars her salary could afford. It may have been a two door, but it was the nicest convertible on the block. Mid twenties, no kids, no crazy ex's, and no nosey mother calling her every five to ten minutes nagging her about having grand children. The only care she had in this world was to see about her puppy 'Bear' and to make sure her home was fully stock with the basic necessities. Cameron lived the life of a bachelorette and she enjoyed every bit of living single. While conversing, one of the employees that had been in the back, walked passed Stephanie and went to the restroom.

"What is that?" Cameron asked curiously as she tried to restrain herself from pointing.

"What?" Looking around the restaurant to see what her friend was cringing over. Crossing her fingers mentally in hopes of it not being some enormous bug.

"On his ear." Placing her hands over her mouth in an attempt to whisper so no one could hear what they were discussing.

Because Stephanie had been working with Reese for several months now, she didn't have to turn and look to know exactly what Cameron was inquiring about.

"You know you wrong for that." Laughing as she kept her head hung low so she wouldn't make eye contact with Reese as he walked by. "I said the same thing when I first met him. I couldn't stop staring."

"I wonder how he got it." Frowning because it was the most ugliest thing she'd ever seen growing on someone's ear.

"I don't know." She chuckled while tapping on the register. "I know some people get them from wearing fake earrings."

"I could see that being the cause." Agreeing with fake jewelry being the cause of the growth if a person had keloid skin. "How long has he been working here?"

"You sure are nosey tonight." Shaking down the register for pennies. "He was here when I got transferred. Why?"

"I think he's kind of cute, but he looks like a dog." Watching Reese as he straightened up the prep table in the back.

"Naa… He's a real nice guy so I've seen. There is one thing I do know about him though." Shifting her body weight to the left.

"Well…" Wondering why Stephanie didn't just come out and say it. Instead of waiting on her to say 'what'.

"He has a little girl and we both know how you feel about dating men with kids."

"True…" *Damn… There goes the little hope he did have.*

"But, you never know. It could be a completely different experience from when you dated Austin." Trying to persuade Cameron not to stereo type every dude she meets with kids. "He could be the one."

"I wonder if he still deals with his baby mom on that level." Rubbing her chin as she considered giving him a chance. As she watched his muscles flex from lifting the containers off the table.

A few years back. Cameron dated a guy by the name of Austin Gray. In the beginning, things were peachy between the two. After school, they'd hang and watch movies. He'd tell her his deepest secrets and she'd share hers. A real life façade. Until one morning before work, Cameron stopped by to drop off some cash he'd asked if he could borrow. Just to hold him over through the weekend and he'd give it back to her that Monday. When she walked up the stairs, she saw a baby stroller parked on the patio. As she reached to ring the door bell, she noticed the door was propped open but the screen was latched. Before she could proceed, a young girl answered and invited her in. Since this was Cameron's first time meeting her. She didn't want to cause a scene because she could've been a relative of his. Later in the visit, she found out that the girl was there for Austin and the money was for their two week old baby's pampers. From that moment on Cameron vowed to never date another guy with children and to do a full investigation before committing to another relationship.

"He says, he doesn't deal with her like that. But we both know how that can go." Wanting to give him the benefit of the doubt. "I kind of believe him, because I hardly ever hear him speak about her." Placing the last twenty count of one's in the register before she jotted down the final numerical value of the entire drawer.

"Umm… Humm…" Resting her chin in the palm of her hand which

was connected to the arm that was resting on the counter. "Do you think he has a girlfriend?"

"Dang girl!" Aggravated from the constant quizzing. "Why don't you ask him for yourself?" Looking crooked eyed at Cameron. "He standing right there!" She shouted as she pointed her clip board in Reese's direction. "I thought you weren't trying to meet no new men, let you tell it. Now look at you. It ain't even been two whole minutes, since you had said you weren't."

Afraid he would be standing directly behind her, Cameron never turned to look. She was as stiff as a statue, cutting Stephanie who was giggling with an evil stare.

"Why you got to be so loud?" She whispered. "I don't want him to know we're talking about him!" Easing her head slightly to the right to use her peripheral view to see if he was paying them any attention. Luckily for her, he had stepped in the freezer.

"I don't be in these employees personal business like that honey. All I know is all I hear and see when I'm on the clock. When I walk outside those doors, I don't think nothing about these people or this place." Placing a wad of money she collected from the registers in a Ziploc bag as she walked toward the safe. "But I can tell you, he lives on that phone of his."

"Pimping I see... Never mind."

Suddenly, Cameron got quiet. Stephanie glanced at her and asked what was wrong but she still said nothing. She felt a swift breeze flow pass her from behind and that's when it dawned on her Reese had walked by. It was amazing how one man could make a woman loose her thought and bite her tongue in his presence. Just the sight of him got her mojo flowing. Reese had swag. Even though he wore the same uniform as his other team mates. It was something unique about the way he chose to wear his. His pants were creased to a tee, like he had them dry cleaned or something. And, you could see his colorful socks poking from underneath the leg of his pants. At first glance you'd think they were mixed match but at a closer view, you could tell they were girl socks. The 'Lashay's' shirt he was wearing had been neatly tucked in the front and flowed freely in the back. Reese had a walk that commanded the room whenever he entered and having that ability was called confidence. He wasn't the best looker, but there was something about him that made Cameron curious.

"Ms. Stephanie," he interrupted.

"Yeah."

"I'm headed out to take the trash to the dumpster."

"Alright, and make sure that back door is shut all the way when you leave out. I don't want nobody trying to come in here while we still in here."

"I will." Smiling because he knew they had been discussing him before he approached them.

Grabbing the plastic bags full of trash from the floor and hauling them off to the back. Reese placed his head phones in his ears to listen to some music while he worked. As soon as he was no longer in sight, Cameron started interrogating again.

"Soooo, his name is Reese." She repeated to Step as she watched him carry the heavy bags through the store.

He knew she had been watching him since she came in and he was intrigued by her interest. Reese never thought he could catch the attention of a woman of Cameron's caliber, but however he did it. He was willing to go with the flow. They danced around one another's stares until his ride came to take him home. And when he was finally out of sight, Cameron felt as if her heart had left with him. Her pulse was elevated and she could feel the steam seeping through her jeans. Within seconds, a glance of him made her moist. She had never experienced this feeling with any man and she wanted to feel more.

"I need to call Albert when I get home," she thought. "My body need some attention and I know he'd get the job done." Thinking he would be the better victim to call to release her frustrations on. "My body is now your body, come and get it. And do with it whatever you like." She serenaded a hymn to herself by Tank.

Carmen had two go to guys she had on speed dial, that were always ready and willing to please whenever she was in need. Dexter Rey was her guy she would call when she wanted company outside of sex. She could definitely count on him to be loving and appreciative, when her pipes needed to be fixed. She knew he would come by with his tool box and plunge which ever hole that was backed up. And her plumbing would flow frequently when he was on the job. Dexter was the lover boy. He didn't just provide the pipe, but he listened to her issues she might've wanted to get off her chest as well. And when it was all said and done, she could be sure to get tucked in tightly and he'd leave her with a kiss on the forehead before he'd go.

Now Albert Greene on the other hand, was quite the opposite. When Cameron had that itch Dexter couldn't seem to scratch and her dill doe batteries were getting weak. She knew she could count on Mr. Greene to bring on the thrill. Cameron and Albert met one evening while she was out late night grocery shopping. It started with your usual small talk, arguing over who gets the last pint of milk and hamburgers or hot dogs. Then, it ended with handcuffs and sex swings. His mother may have named him Albert, but he damn sure didn't act like one. He wowed the socks off this girl their first go round and he'd became a regular addiction ever since.

"Step!"

"What's up?" Coming out of the back office with another chart in her hands.

"I'm about to head home. Come lock up." Gathering her things as she prepared her finger to push the number three down on her key pad.

"I thought you were spending the night with me tonight." Wanting to know why she had the sudden change of mind.

"I have to go to work in the morning and I can't remember if I left enough food out for Bear." Knowing good and well she left him two full bowls of dog food and water out, because she knew she wasn't coming back. She just wanted an excuse to press send.

"You can go to work from my house. Plus, Rico out of town and he won't be back until Monday. Therefore, we can sit up and have girl talk like we usually do without any interruptions." Hoping Cameron would agree to come over so she wouldn't have to be alone.

"Okay, I'd come." Sucking her teeth under her breath because she had gotten herself roused up mentally for Albert to conquer her body physically. "I guess Bear can make it till 2 p.m. with what I left for him already."

Punching in a few numbers on the register. Stephanie got angry because the manager that worked the shift before hers, didn't finish her work. Which meant, she had to add it to her work load. Stephanie wouldn't have had a problem with finishing it if she was given a heads up about it first. But, most of the managers that worked at Lashay's weren't considerate enough to consider others.

"I would've been out of here if Kareem lazy ass didn't skip out on her counts." Slamming her clip board on the counter as she referenced the register.

"How much you got left?"

"I'm finished now!" Staring at the screen. "I was just saying we could have been gone if she would've done her damn job!"

"Oh." Witnessing Stephanie's nose flare up as the veins in her forehead played Marco Polo, shifting positions with the loose skin that formed ridges in her face.

"You can go ahead and get in the car, while I set this alarm real quick." Stephanie advised after she punched in a few more clicks on the front register, which caused a long slip of paper to print out.

As she turned out the lights, her stomach started to growl. She had been at 'Lashay's' all day and had forgotten to feed herself. Stephanie continued to lock up before she proceeded to walk over to Cameron's car.

"I need to stop by 'McHomand's' before we go to the house. I haven't ate all day and I'm starving right now." Rubbing her aching tommy.

"That's fine with me. I could use a snack myself." Rocking to the music that was playing softly in her background. As she reached for the volume nozzle to turn it up. "That's why I like you, you, you yeah," she sang.

"Who is that? I like that song."

"This new artist name J-dro. My home girl Danielle manages him and she gave me a cd to check it out for her."

"What's the name of it?" Nodding her head as she listened to the words.

Rambling through her back seat. Cameron pulled out a big black cd case and flipped through the slots until she saw a gold and brown cover with a Cadillac emblem embedded on the front.

"The album is 'Lac Muzik' and the song is called 'You'. If you want a copy, I can call her up and ask her for another copy for you."

"Yeah, how much is it?"

"Don't worry about the price. I can get it free. But if you want to hear it sooner, just download it off the internet."

"Cool beans… Now let's go get this burger before I faint out here."

As the girls rode through the drive-thru to place their orders. Cameron couldn't believe how long the line was. McHomand's was jumping late night and it was half past 1 a.m. when they arrived. You'd think people would be at home this time of the morning, but I guess not in this neck of the woods. Because of the time and the fact that she had to drive all the way to Roswell rd. for work at 5 a.m. Cameron decided she wouldn't go to sleep. She figured if she stayed up and chat until it was time for her to go, her body would go into over drive and push through the sleep. When they got to the house. The girls laughed and joked about past run-ins they've had with some of the crazy people they'd meet at the club, back in their teenage years. Both were a bit wild and adventurous; any idea was a good idea back then.

"You remember that time we went to that club on the eastside and you got so drunk that you tried to talk to that dude who's girlfriend was there with her cousins?"

"Hell yeah."

"What was the name of that club again?"

"The Spot."

"Yeah, that's it. That bitch didn't see that bottle coming that night." Stephanie laughed.

"I know right." Reminiscing on the night her and Dexter met. "Till this day I got his number programed in my speed dial as #2."

"Say what!" Choking on a piece of hamburger she hadn't finished breaking down. "You mean to tell me you're still doing that man?"

"Girl yeah! Where you been?" Searching at the bottom of her bag to see if there were any stray fries hiding behind the napkins. "How you think I've been getting my rocks off? I just know you didn't think I was celibate for four months."

"I don't know," she shrugged. Stunned by her scandalous friend news. "I thought you were energizing it." She blurted as juice flew out her nose. While she attempted to lean forward to pound her chest and catch her breath through all the laughing.

"That too!" Cameron joked. "You remember seeing what happened to that girl on the news that the owner was dating?" Squeezing ketchup on the last fry she found hiding out in the bag.

"Yeah, that was sad."

"I know, I wonder what made her do it."

"I don't know, but I know the owner hasn't been there lately. I heard through the grapevine he planning on selling because it brings back to many memories for him."

"I heard he was selling because some people were after him."

"What…"

"Yeah honey."

After they ate. The girls continued to joke about random events that were taking place in their ever present lives. Looking down at her watch, Cameron noticed time had flown by mighty fast and she had to get a move on it if she wanted to make it to work on time.

"Girl, I got to get out of here. It's 4:55 a.m."

"For real?"

"Yeah honey. I'd text you when I get home after work."

"Make sure you call me and make sure you do some snooping for me on that neighbor of yours."

"Ain't nobody got time for that! Bye!"

"Lock the bottom lock!" Stephanie yelled.

"Alright."

CRAZY MAN

When Cameron got to work, she wished she'd called out prior to her arrival. The morning started off slow and it smelt like rain. By her being up the entire night, dealing with customers wasn't the issue. The annoyance would come from her co-workers. Just the thought of stepping foot in that place put a sour taste in her mouth. Seeing all the smiling faces awaiting her to return the gesture and the morning salutations drove her nuts. Having to hold your true feelings about a person on the inside to maintain your financial stability is a struggle. And Cameron had to find the strength to muscle through it everyday.

"Here goes nothing." She grunted before she flung the door open. Sighing as she held her head high and placed one foot in front of the other.

"Welcome to 'Brandy's'!" The crew yelled. None of them were at the front counter. It was a habit for everyone to say it when they heard the door alarm chime. One of the new policies the company started enforcing to make the customers feel more welcome.

"Hey Cameron!" A perky voice came from behind.

"Oh, hey Tonya." Turning to face her as she came from one of the side booths in the lobby. "What you doing back there?"

"I was cleaning off a couple tables." Shaking the rag she was holding to get the crumbs off. "We had a family come in and they had some bay bays." She joked. "What's new?"

"Dang, can I not clock in first before you start drilling me about my personal." Pulling her backpack off to lay it in the cubby underneath the television.

"You can't multitask?" Standing in the sanitary station to wash her hands.

"Yes I can smart ass. But, I'd prefer to tell you after I get my drive-thru station prepped for the lunch rush." Grabbing her time slip off the printer. "Have y'all been busy so far?"

"Not really. We had that one family that just left and I want to say maybe six customers before that." Counting the tickets that were left on the order screen. "You know Saturday mornings pretty slow around here. Either they at some type of sports practice for the kids or they're still in bed." Opening a few to-go bags to place coupons in them. "The real money don't come until noon."

"Has the truck come by yet to drop off the bread?"

"Yeah, the driver left the bread stacked by the back door."

"Outside?"

"Umm hum… You know how they do. Enough of this business talk, tell me what really went down last weekend. You know I only see you twice a week girl. I need all the juice."

"It went alright." Pulling the plastic off a sleeve of cups so she could stack them next to the drink machine.

"Anything juicy happen?" Staring Cameron in the mouth to make sure she didn't miss not one word.

"Yeah, but I wouldn't call it juicy." Cameron teased. "I do have a little something, something to spill."

"Hold that thought." She advised as she eagerly rushed to open the register drawer. "Count this money down first and tell me when you've finished. I don't want no distractions outside of customers, when you get started."

If something happens to Cameron over the weekend. Usually it flows through the following week. She had always lived an interesting life. Even in her adolescent years. If life could be viewed on primetime television. You'd find several seductive episodes that will have you hooked no matter what season you'd start from. The television headline would read 'Drama' and Cameron would play the leading role. Filled with action and guaranteed to have viewers sitting on the edge of their seats begging for more. It's one thing to live a suspenseful life, but it takes a special someone to tell the story and make the listener feel as if they were there.

"Okay, I'm ready." Motioning for Tonya to come back in the corner.

"Ooo… Let me grab some fries." Excited as a mild chill came over her body, which caused an unknown amount of bumps to arise. Scooping up a scoop full of curly fries. Tonya slid the hot, crunchy, peppery potatoes in a container and flung the utensil back in it's hoister. She grabbed the nearest bottle of honey mustard and prepared her feast. "I'm ready."

"Remember I told you the last time I saw you, me and Pooda was supposed to go to the park last weekend right."

"Umm hum…" Chopping down on the first victimized spud, which coincidentally had been singled out from the rest of the batch.

"Apparently, I didn't know they were having a parade in the area I wanted to go. So, when we linked up. He asked me what park I wanted to have the picnic at and I was like 'Beadmonte'."

"Right."

"But, as time got closer for us to meet at the station he started acting funny. And was the main one talking about feeding ducks." Sucking her teeth as she remembered the details of that crazy weekend. "So I asked my mom if she could drop me off at the station because I didn't want to drive my car down there. Plus, he hadn't seen my car yet."

"How you manage to do that?"

"We met on the train one night I was coming home from work. I wanted to see if he'd continue to like me without knowing what I had."

"Okay." Rolling her eyes because she didn't see the meaning behind Cam's plan. Her car was pretty fancy but Tonya didn't see the need in hiding the fact that she had it.

"We gets to the station and I still had to wait."

"Why?" Fumbling with the remaining fries she had left, before she started licking the sauce off her fingers so she could open another pack of honey mustard.

"Cause he was still in the car with his cousin!" Feeling as if she was about to blow a gasket. "You know how I feel about being on time."

"How long did you have to wait?" Laughing as she watched Cameron's cheeks turn rosy pink.

"Not that long. He eventually walked up the ramp."

"Dag, I'm almost out of fries." Looking down in the quarter empty container. "This sounds like it's just about to get good and I'm almost out of freaking fries." Shaking the box to toss the contents around as a mixing technique.

"Anyway, he saw me before I saw him. But, when I did see him. I was like 'Damn'." Smiling as she continued. "He looked good girl…" Using a deep tone.

"What…"

"Hell yeah…" Leaning on the counter top as she crossed her ankles and blushed.

Even though Cameron was telling Tonya what had happened. Her imagination took her back to the exact day and moment when the event took place, which made her feel as if she was reliving the moment all over again. The setting around her was erased and she was standing in the middle of the train station staring Anthony in the face. But, she called him her 'Pooda'.

"Hey."

"What's up." She greeted him with an unwelcoming tone.

"My bad I was late." Holding his head down so he wouldn't have to look her in the eyes.

"I been told you I was on the way and I still managed to beat you here. When I said I was coming, I hadn't even left the house yet."

"I can't control how fast or slow people drive." Staring Cameron in the eyes, wanting to smile but he didn't want to make her angrier then she already was, admiring her left dimple she tried to force away.

"But you knew ahead of time!"

"Man, where's my hug?" Opening his arms as he awaited her to step in.

Giving in to his gesture. Cameron wrapped her arms around his neck and melted. Anthony was strong but his grip was gentle. He could smell traces of vanilla scented perfume on her neck and smiled as he inhaled the fumes.

"So…" Exhaling to exhaust all the oxygen he inhaled. "Have you made up your mind about where you wanted to go yet?"

"I would like to go to the park like we discussed in the beginning."

"What's so special about you and the park anyway?" Wanting to convince her to change her mind. He figured if he complained enough, she'd agree to go somewhere else. Anthony didn't have a problem with going initially. It wasn't until he found out about the parade that caused him to change his mind.

"Nothing special." She advised. "I really want to go so we can talk more and get to know each other better in a more intimate setting. You know I'm a romantic." She teased.

As Anthony and Cameron made their way up the escalator. Cameron couldn't help but notice the man that stood before her. Anthony was nothing like the men she was use to dealing with. His body was covered in tattoos and his hair was shaven around the edges except in the middle. Because of his unique style, he chose to have index finger length dreads on the crown. At first glance it was frightening but after several minutes the look would grow on you. The train was docked when they finally reached the platform. Pretending to be a gentlemen, Anthony stepped to the side to allow Cameron to take the inside seat while he sat in the outer.

"Why you looking at me like that?" She asked.

"Is it bothering you?" He chuckled.

"In a way it is. You're making me feel like I have butterflies in my tummy." Blushing while looking down in the palm of her sweaty hands, wondering what he could've been thinking when he was staring at her.

"What you nervous about?"

"I don't know," ashamed. Wishing she'd kept her mouth shut. "Just stop looking at me!" Turning to look in the opposite direction, trying to focus her attention on the trees that passed her window.

"I can't help it." He admitted as his cheeks lite up like a tree on Christmas day. "Your eyes are so beautiful."

"Thank you." With her head still turned in the opposite direction.

"We can go anywhere you want today except Beadmonte Park." Resting his fitted cap on his knee.

He thought it was only fair she saw the real him. Therefore, he took his cap off when he first entered the station. If she was going to date him, he wanted it to be the real thing.

"Do you have something against that park?" Looking Anthony directly in the eyes. "Why can't we go there?"

"Ugh… If that's where you want to go, then we can go."

Satisfied with herself after winning the argument. Cameron reached over and placed her hands in his. Nervous because they had just met a day ago. She tried to hide the way she felt, but the latter noticed the obvious. The ride was sweet and romantic but was cut short because they had arrived at their destination faster then anticipated. When Cameron and Anthony exited the train, neither of them spoke a word. Instead, they walked hand in hand till they reached the street.

"Wait right here real quick. I need a smoke." Pulling his cigarette pack from the inside of his back pocket.

"The sign says no smoking." Pointing to the blue and white sign nailed to the wall of the train station. "You can stand over on that side of the street or you can smoke while we walk, but you can't light up right here."

"Walking and smoking is not an option. It's to damn hot out here for all that shit."

"Excuse me… I was just making a suggestion."

"Next time, think before you speak." Struggling to strike the match on the crumbled up scratch strip on the back.

"What!" Cameron shouted as she watched the wrinkled cigarette wiggle in between his lips.

"Man, fuck this shit!" Throwing the stick down.

"You know what! I don't have to put up with this from you!" She said as she made her way back to the gate. "I don't even know you like that! I'm done!" Leaving Anthony standing by himself on the sidewalk.

"And then what happened?" Tonya asked.

"You know that fool started going off on me."

"Say what!" Shocked from the news of his reaction. "Why he do that? He don't even know you like that."

"Child... He didn't care! We were arguing like we'd been together for years. Talking about he don't want to go down there and why we can't hang at the mall. The thing that pissed me off the most about the whole situation is the fact that he waited until we got all the way down there to say he didn't want to stay. I might've been ok with the change if he'd said it in the beginning. Instead of waiting till I spent my bus fair."

"Did y'all stay?"

"Naw, I left!" Cameron fussed as she reached for the headset that was hanging on the wall over the computer screen. "I went home and didn't look back!" Swapping the battery out. "And had the nerve to text and ask me where I was! I cursed him clean out for that mess!"

"Men these days. What do they be thinking?" Throwing the container in the trash. As she shook her head while she pushed the soap dispenser button in the sanitary station.

"They don't."

After several hours of cleaning and taking orders. Cameron passed out her last bag and thought to restock for the next shift when she heard the ring tone sound from her cellular phone. Since it was near time for her to get off, she figured it was Step calling to see what was on the schedule for that evening. Usually Cameron would work the morning shift on Saturdays and then they'd go out. By her not getting any sleep the previous night, she wanted to do just that. So, she ignored the call. The door bell sounded and the entire crew greeted the guest.

"It's just me!" Mrs. Pam yelled.

"Thank you Lord!" Cameron shouted. Happy to see her relief had arrived and she was on time for the first time. "I got everything stocked and ready for you."

"Aren't you the perkiest of them all today. How was business so far?" Punching in on the time clock.

"Steady for now. And hell yeah I'm happy! You're on time! Which means I can leave on time, duh! Who wouldn't be excited?" Grabbing her bag from the cubby she placed it in when she first arrived. "I'd see y'all later!"

"Don't leave yet Cam!" Tonya shouted as she slid a sandwich down the shoot from back line. "I haven't counted down your register yet!"

"Well you need to hurry up then! People got things to do around here!"

"Don't rush me!" Pulling the gloves off her hands as she came around the corner. "What's another five minutes?"

"Five extra minutes I could be using for sleep. If anything's missing, call me. I got to go." Pushing the door open. "And make sure you clock me out too!"

Stepping in the foyer, you could smell a strong fowl mixture of dog poop and urine clouding the room. Even though she'd only been gone for a few hours, the damage would take days to repair. Having a cat was nothing compared to having a puppy for a pet. The difference between the two clearly lies in the concept of kitty litter and grass. Cameron tried paper training the pup, but he didn't catch on as fast as she assumed he would. Her efforts in leaving him newspapers to do his business on went down the drain after seeing shreds of the daily news scattered all over the floor. There wasn't a point of getting angry and calling out for him about it, because he greeted her at the door with non-stop licking and tail wagging.

"You would be happy to see me when you know your butt was about to get in trouble." Watching him jump up and down on her leg, begging to be picked up. "If I wasn't tired right now, it would be me and you mister." Squatting down to rub him. "You're so fluffy and so cute though. Who could be mad at that little face?" Using a soft playful tone as she lifted him in her arms to kiss his pink nose. "I hope you didn't make to big of a mess for mommy while she was away. I'll tend to it after my nap." Ignoring the huge pile of shit she saw sitting next to her caramel colored couch.

Using the tip of her foot to pull off her sneaker from the rear. Cameron peeled off her work shoes leaving the socks in the soles and flopped in bed clothes and all. She rested her head on the soft, plush pillow that had a frost to it; from the lack of occupancy the night before. Tossing a blanket over her body as she wiggled ten toes underneath to create a comfortable space to place them. Cameron's eyes hadn't been shut for a whole fifteen minutes, when she heard a loud bang coming from the other side of her bedroom window. Frightened, because she wasn't use to hearing such a ruckus in her six years of living in this particular neighborhood. She leaped out of bed, ducked low to the floor, and eased her body near the panel. When she reached the curtain. She stood half her height and peered out the side of the blinds.

After Cameron figured she was completely in spy mode. She cracked the curtains well enough so she'd have a clear view of her new neighbor, pacing back and forth in his yard on the telephone. As a safety precaution, she had double paned windows installed before she moved in. Which were now a pain in the ass because she couldn't make out anything he was saying. The instillation may have been sound proof, but the walls were as thin as a sheet of paper. Cameron wasn't usually a nosey neighbor, but, before she could retire back to her California King. A white Suburban swooped in his driveway and three dudes hopped out. Turk, Murf, and Paul. Which she would soon learn the new resident 'Bobby', was the ring leader.

SOMETHING'S OFF

Bobby Williams was a young gangster born and raised in the heart of Compton. Because of the depth of gang violence in his neighborhood. He was pressured into leaving the city because a lot of people wanted what he had. Raised in the streets, the only thing he knew how to do was survive. Nickel and diming it to make ends meet wasn't his forte. Being able to purchase things without having to worry about the price, was more up his alley. Bobby called all the shots and made every out of state transaction to make sure he continued to sustain a six figure income bi-weekly. There was only four people he trusted on this earth; his best friend Paul. Murf and Turk, who were identical twins that grew up with him on the block. And, his only breathing sibling Mo. Mo was younger then Bobby and more domesticated, but, she was extremely over protective of him as well.

"I just got a call from some dude that claims he got Mo."

"You know I'd take care of that problem for you. Just say the word." Murf stated as he revealed the glock he had hidden on his right hip tucked underneath his shirt.

"Naa… I got something special in mind." Paul suggested.

"Let's take this in the house. Your neighbor looking at us." Murf advised, while blowing a kiss at the window Cameron was peeping from.

When she realized all eyes were on her. She hurried and turned loose the blinds and backed away from the window as if she had seen a ghost. It was bad enough that she was being nosey, but getting caught doing so made it seem even worse.

Leading the group in the house. Bobby instructed Paul to lock the door and motioned for Turk to shut the blinds. They were about to get down to business and he wanted to be certain none of his new neighbors were snooping around witnessing anything accidentally. Having casualties over a mishap he could have prevented, was not something he planned on worrying about. Paul pulled out a package about the size of a brick from between his legs. That sat in the seat of his jeans and placed it on the kitchen counter top.

"Where's the baking soda?" Turk asked as he tied the back of the grey apron he slid on.

"Look in the box by the sink that got 'seasonings' written on it." Bobby pointed. "Roll that blunt 'G'!" He shouted at Murf who was already sitting on the couch breaking down the leaves.

"What's the plan Money?" Paul asked. Leaning up against the island watching Turk stir the contents slowly in the glass pot that was simmering on the stove.

"Roll up on their set." Shaking his head as he slow dragged on a cigarette. "And trash bag them fools." Exhaling as water flooded his eyes.

Bobby couldn't believe someone kidnapped his sister. Every night since the drive-by that claimed the life of his mother and elder brother. He would wake up in a cold sweat from a nightmare of him and Mo being next. With one hand on his 357 and the moonlight shinning on his bare chest, as he'd look around the room to make sure no one was hiding in the shadows. Bobby wasn't afraid of death. But, the thing that spooked him the most was the thought of his past coming back to haunt him. He felt his karma came from the death of his family, but it seems that tragedy was only the beginning.

"Once you get those cookies broke down, I need you to check and see if anyone from the block saw or heard anything. I don't care if all they saw was the back of dude's head. I want to know if he had dreads, braids, temp, or a bald greasy ass scalp. Any news is good news."

"I got you Money." Turk confirmed.

"I can't believe they saw me." She whispered to herself as she bit down on her nails. Shocked because she was caught being the one thing that plucked her nerves the most about people, nosey.

Bear was being destructive but Cameron paid him no mind. She sat there in fear for her life because she didn't know anything regarding what they were discussing and she wasn't sure if they knew she didn't hear anything or not. Since it's obvious the fellas saw her looking. She wasn't sure of how she should act when they saw her out in the street.

"The man just moved over here and he's already causing problems." She said angrily as she crawled back towards the window to see if the coast was clear.

Because she didn't want to embarrass herself again, Cameron peeped from the bottom of the blinds this time around. When she got a full view of his front yard, no one was caught standing on the porch or sitting in the cars. Glancing to her left to check the back lawn, she was relieved no one was standing there either.

"I ain't staying here tonight!" She stated while brushing her knees off as she arose from the plush carpet. "I'm about to pack my shit and get out of here."

As Cameron pulled her suitcase from the top shelf of her closet, she heard a beeping noise coming from outside. It sounded as if someone was setting the alarm on their vehicle and she wanted to know exactly who it was. Curious of what was going on out there, she dropped the suitcase and scurried to the window. When she stuck her finger through the blinds to create enough space where one eyeball could peep through. She rolled it around, but saw no one.

"Dag, I missed them!" As she continued to look, a sudden knock came at her front door. "Ahh, shit!" Turning around as fast as she could. Watching Bear run out the room barking as if he was going to answer it for her. "That's them!" Coming to terms with the fact that she had no other choice but to answer it because they already knew she was home. "Who is it?"

"It's Step! Open the door girl! I got to pee!" She yelled as she rocked side to side holding her crotch.

"Boy, am I glad to see you." Pulling Stephanie by the arm in the house as she stuck her head out the door to see if anyone was looking.

"What done climbed up your skirt?" Running down the hall in an attempt to make it to the toilet.

"Shh… Keep your voice down!" Shushing Stephanie while she bolted the door and slid the latch on.

"Why your house smell like boo-boo?" Tearing off a couple sheets of tissue from the roll while she glanced around the restroom to make sure she didn't see any poo poo piles laying around.

"Bear did it in the living room while I was at your house. Speaking of, I'm coming over for a couple days."

"What!" Shocked by the way Cameron felt she could volunteer herself to spend the night. Like she knew she didn't have anything else going on that night.

"Yeah girl, I'll fill you in when we get there. But right now I need you to help me pack."

"I like your nerve!" Objecting while she washed her hands. "How you just gon' volunteer yourself to come over my place? I didn't extend you another invitation. That was for yesterday only ma'am. What are you going to do about that dog if you plan on coming my way?"

"He coming with me." Shoving her tooth brush and tooth paste in her knapsack as quickly as possible.

"Like hell he is! I got cats!"

"They'll be alright. I can put him on the patio."

"Something must've happened. Is that Dexter guy girl friend sending you threatening messages again?" Shaking the water off her hands while she laughed.

"Naa… It's a bit more complicated then that." Shoving some random panties and socks in the bag.

"Well, tell me what's up." Leaning on the bedroom door post. "Because you can't bring that dog over my house without having a good excuse on why he has to tag along." Using her foot to tease Bear as he acted as if he was attacking it.

Cameron knew she wasn't going to be able to leave the house without having to explain to Stephanie what caused her to want to rush and leave. She felt it would be better if they could discuss it on their way out, but she saw she wasn't getting out that door without passing Step first. Even if Stephanie said no to her coming over, Cameron still could go crash at her moms.

"I was laying in the bed about to take my nap, when I heard this loud noise coming from outside. As I got up to see what it was, this tuck pulled up in the neighbors yard and some dudes jumped out."

"What…"

"Yeah…" Looking at Stephanie posted on the wall all surprised and engulfed in what she had to say.

"What happened after they got out?"

"They were standing around talking but one of them saw me looking and blew a kiss at me. Then, they all turned and saw me looking out my window. After that, they went in the house." Zipping her bag.

"And then what happened?"

"I started packing my stuff and you pulled up."

"Are you serious?" Confused because she didn't see any reason for Cameron to be nervous enough to leave her home. "You got to be kidding me."

"Yeah, I'm serious. What do you mean?" Rolling her suitcase down the hall as she held Bear with her left arm.

"You're antsy because some dudes saw you looking out your window, of your house." Using her nail to pick her teeth. "Who knows. They may have thought you were checking them out. You did say one blew a kiss at you right?"

"Yeah, he did." Feeling as if she was over reacting thanks to mother Stephanie.

"Okay then scary Mary! Duh!"

"You're right. Maybe I am over reacting a little bit."

"A little bit! Hell, a little lot!" She joked.

"Now that I'm feeling like a complete idiot. What brings you over this way?"

Letting Bear go as she slid her suitcase up against the wall. Cameron felt embarrassed that she'd over exaggerated the situation, but it never crossed her mind that they could have thought she was checking them out. Following Stephanie in the kitchen, she couldn't help but wonder what the fellas were talking about as she tuned in and out of her conversation with Step.

"I know you said you were going to call but since I was in the area, I swung on by."

"Well, I guess since you're here and it looks like I'm not getting that nap after all. What you want to do?" Taking a bite out of a left over sub sandwich she had stashed in the refrigerator.

"I want to go see a movie if you're up to it."

"Cool, but let's go to the nail salon first. I need a fill in bad girl." Looking down at her chewed up cuticles.

"That's fine, and I need to stop by 'Styles' to check out some of the new arrivals. I remember one of the clerks told me last time I was there 'Shine's' fall collection premier this weekend. I need to see what good pieces I can get before the crowd rush in."

Fall has always been crowned as one of the best seasons in fashion for centuries. Designers prepare their teams to create extreme masterpieces to compete in this competitive industry every year before the line is expected to premier. During this opportune time of the year. Industry leaders get to experiment with different shades and pattern modifications to show off their creativity to the public. The best sales start at the end of the summer. You have the back to school discounts, tax free weekend, black Friday madness, holiday sales, and the end of the year clearance sale on every product created in that year.

"I need 75% off tags on every piece of fabric hanging on those three racks in the front." Pointing to the front of the store. "I don't want to see not one piece of cloth from last season hanging in this boutique come the end of the month." She demanded. "The other six racks need to have half off tags plastered on them from top to bottom. And should be pushed toward the front as well, to grab the customers attention." Reaching over the counter. "My fall line premiers this weekend and everything in this store has to go." Handing out mark down guns to her two flunkies. "Let's work!"

Laura and Antoinette were tired from the previous night because they had been out partying the entire time. Since Shelly gave Nette the weekend off from babysitting, she took advantage of the freedom. Nette was usually on babysitting duty because it was Shelly's clever way of getting out of paying for a sitter. What better way to save money than to force your baby sister into doing it for you for free. Since Shelly didn't have the extra funds coming in to compensate the extra expense added to the medical bills she was still recovering from. She figured Nette owed her. Ding dong. The sensor chimed to notify the employees when a customer had arrived.

"Welcome to Styles!" Laura yelled from the back end of the boutique.

"Hey honey!" Stephanie greeted back. "What's new?" Smiling as she adjusted her purse on her arm.

"Ohh, hey boo!" Looking up at Stephanie as she approached, while sliding a hanger in the neck of the blouse she was holding. "What brings you girls in my neck of the woods today?" Tagging the blouse with a 75% off sticker.

"We plan on hitting a matinee, but Cam wanted to get her nails done first. Plus, I wanted to stop by to see what you guys had on these racks that I could use for tonight." Reaching out to give her a hug.

Shifting the rest of the shirts she was holding under her left arm pit, while gripping her discount gun in her right hand. Laura stretched her arms as wide as she could to welcome her friends embrace.

"Well, you know the new stuff don't arrive until Friday. So right now we're marking all the summer stuff down, to make room for the delivery."

Looking over Stephanie's shoulders to make sure Shelly didn't catch her lollygagging on the clock.

"Why you look so paranoid?" Placing her hand over her chest to calm herself in case someone was standing behind her.

"You know Suella don't play around about fraternizing on her dime."

"Where's that old prune anyway?" Giggling as she joked about Shelly being a stick in the mud.

"She's in the back." Laura laughed as she hung another shirt.

"Well, I just dropped in to make sure the clothes will be here Friday. Our movie starts at 8:00 p.m. so we need to be on our way." Looking back at Cameron who was flipping through the 50% off rack.

"Alright then girl, call me."

"I will." She assured her as she whistled at Cameron and motioned for her to come on.

As the girls walked down the strip. They couldn't help the urge to stop at every window they saw that had a huge red sign hanging in it with white letters that spelled 'sale' on it. It felt like Christmas in the summer, but neither one of them wouldn't dare touch their purses. For they knew the better deals would come that weekend. The smell of alcohol and nail polish remover was so strong, you'd think the girls had already arrived. But they were only two stores down.

"What color you plan on getting?" Stephanie asked as she struggled to decide between French or the American tip.

"I'm getting midnight plum with gold sparkles on top of my wedding finger. How about you?"

"I don't know yet, but that sounds cute."

"Yeah, I hope it comes out the way I envisioned it. If not, I'm going to switch it to all white." Flipping her hands front to back as she tried to imagine her nails with plum tips.

After having arrived at their destination, Cameron took one good look around the room and concluded this was going to be a hell of a wait. There were no vacant seats in the waiting area and all of the booths were filled with paying customers. When they left Stylez it was 5:17 p.m. and she knew if they sat longer than twenty five minutes waiting to get seen, they'd surely miss the movie. But, if she didn't get her nails done today. She'd have to wait another week and a half before she could make time to do so.

"Hello." A guy standing at about a good four inches greeted them as they blocked the entrance. "What would you like?" He asked showing all thirty two as he bowed in their presence.

"Two full-sets with Mani's and Pedi's for both."

"Sure, sure. I'll do for you. Come with me."

As he led the ladies to the pedicure chairs, it seemed like all eyes were on them as they passed. Every eyeball in the salon followed as they walked.

"Xiū zhǐjiǎ hé xiūjiǎo." He told the employees that awaited to service them. "Ming Ming will take good care of you. What ever you like, she will do for you."

"Thank you, Lee." Cameron thanked as she bowed her head out of respect to return his gesture.

"Did it seem like everybody was looking at us to you?" Stephanie asked while pulling off her shoes.

"Yeah, I was about to ask you the same thing. What's up with that?"

"I don't know but I hope she don't take forever and a day on our nails, so we won't miss this flick."

"I heard that." Throwing her hand in the air to give Stephanie a high five as they laughed.

Twenty minutes into the massage she was receiving on her back from the chair and her feet courtesy of Ming Ming. Cameron couldn't take her mind off the events that took place earlier that day with the new neighbor. She considered the assumption Stephanie made, but her gut told her to believe otherwise. Something was up with those guys and she wasn't going to rest until she figured out what.

"Are you sure you think my neighbor may have thought I was checking them out and not being nosey?" Focusing her attention on Stephanie as she witnessed her eyes roll.

"Please don't ruin my miniature orgasmic session with your frightful tendencies." She said as the vibrations from the chair caused her voice to buzz as if she was humming her words. "They ain't stunting you. Hopefully, he done forgot all about your peeping tom ass and introduces himself the next time he sees you."

"I hope you're right." Rubbing her hand across her forehead.

"Of course I am. One day we're going to look back on this day and laugh. Watch and see what I tell you. If not, I owe you a trip to Hawaii." She laughed.

"Deal."

LIGHTS OUT

It was three in the morning and everybody on the block was asleep. Bobby propped open his screen and rushed to the middle of his driveway as he awaited the white suburban to back in. Using a flash light to guide the fellas in because he didn't want to make any disturbing noises. Bobby silently directed the truck in and popped open the hatch.

"Let's get this mother fucker in the house before one of my neighbors witness anything." He whispered in the window. "I'd hate for there to be bad blood between any of us and I haven't had a chance to get settled yet." He continued as he dragged the black trash bag closer to him. "Grab the legs and I'll get her arms." Directing Turk towards the lighter end of the load.

As the fellas carried her body in the house. Paul parked the vehicle at the end of the driveway so they could have a clear view of any passer byers. Because of the heavy rain, they tracked mud all over Bobby's shampooed carpet. You could hear the sound of water being squished between a sock and the sole of each one of their combat boots.

"Damn it!"

"What's wrong B?" Turk asked as he stopped in the middle of the hall carrying a third of 169 pounds.

"We done jacked up my carpet." He whispered.

"No worries Cinderella. My girl got some stuff that will have your floor looking good as new."

"Cool, cool. Let's take her to the back. I covered the windows with tape, so no one will be able to see her back there."

Because Bobby's home was a ranch style construction, he didn't have the luxury of having a basement. Therefore he had to make due with the space he did have available to him. If at any point it ever crossed his mind he'd be holding someone hostage and torturing them in the comforts of his own home. He would have been certain to have that amenity as an attachment.

Shoving their victim in a wooden chair that sat in the middle of the room. The guys wasted no time in regard to tying her down. Paul came in and pulled a cord which was hanging next to the light bulb that was connected to the ceiling. 'Clink, clink'. The sound of the cord made as he yanked. The brightness of the light beamed on Tami as she cracked the lids of her eyes in an attempt to stare her enemies in theirs. You could tell by the rays of the light this was a fresh bulb, never before used until now. Beads of sweat formed on Tami's forehead as she wrestled with the tape that bonded her wrists together behind her seating.

"Let me go!" She mumbled underneath the sticky duck tape that trapped her lips together like a fly to waxed paper. Rocking her body left from right using all of her energy to try and free her ankles which were strapped to the legs of the chair as well. "Let me go!" She welled as her eyes watered from the sight of four men standing before her, soak and wet from the severe thunder storm they were now sheltered from.

"What are we going to do with her?" Murf asked.

"Leave her here till the morning. I'd think of a way to make this bitch scream by then." Bobby replied as he felt an ache in his heart from all the hatred he felt from what she'd done to him. "Just because you freed my sister, doesn't mean you'll get the same compassion from me." He said as they locked eyes. "You're going to feel every bit of pain you've caused me while my sister was gone." He promised. "You can bet your life on that." Biting his bottom lip with a devilish smirk on his face as he turned faced the door. "Turn the light out on her and let her face her demons."

"Night, night rabbit." Murf teased. "Tricks aren't just for kids." Sticking his tongue between two fingers as he flicked it up and down.

"Dude! Come on!" Turk demanded as he slapped his brother in the back of his head. "We got somewhere to be!"

After shutting the door. Turk informed Bobby they had other endeavors to indulge in and they had to make it to the destination within the hour. Since Paul rode with them, he had to say his goodbyes also.

"I'd call you later in the morning to see what the move is regarding shorty back there."

"Alright man." Dapping Paul up. "The only thing I want to do right now is get some rest and thank the man upstairs for bringing Mo back in one piece."

"I hear that my dog." Rubbing his chin as he reflected on the scare they had earlier that day when they first found out Mo was gone.

"I'd check y'all goons later." Following behind his friends to lock up.

"For sure." Paul stated as he jogged sideways down the steps.

"Word!" Murf agreed.

"Word…"

GOOD MORNING

Friday had finally come but Cameron wasn't eager to get out of bed. The sun had reached it's peek and she had been laying there since she laid down the night before. The postman dropped by to leave some mail in her box, two hours prior to her opening her eyes. And, to her dismay. Bear had been running vigorously throughout her home, knocking over everything that wasn't nailed to the floor. Rolling over until her feet reached the carpet. Cameron glanced at her alarm clock which read 12:02 p.m. and slide into her slippers.

"Damn…" She grumbled. "I need to let that dog out before he get a chance to mess all over my carpet again." She said as she wiped the snot from underneath her nose.

Reaching for the hanger that was hooked to the back of her bedroom door. Cameron wrestled with her oversized night gown until she got her robe properly wrapped around her body.

"Bear!" She called out to her miniature poodle. "Come on, so you can go potty!" She yelled. "I'm not in the mood for cleaning this morning!" Looking over her left shoulder into the dinning area where she saw a little chocolate monster, tussling with one of the pillows he'd dragged off the couch that sat in the living room.

"If you don't get your little butt..." She threatened as he shot in between her legs. Forcing her knees to bend from the impact of him hitting the bottom of her silk gown. Soaring over the four steps attached to her porch. Until he landed in a cool patch of grass.

"Boy! I ought to..." Giggling as she watched her playful pup dash across her lawn like it was his first time experiencing dirt. "What am I going to do with you?"

While standing on her patio. A school of birds caught Cameron's attention. As they crossed the light blue sky. Which distracted her from noticing her neighbor sitting on his patio smoking a cigarette. Bobby watched her as she gazed at the birds and puffed as he studied her while she walked to her mailbox.

"Good morning," she waved. Startled when she noticed him rocking in his rocking chair.

"Top of the morning!" He yelled back at her in a deep unauthentic tone.

"It looks like we're going to have a beautiful day today, huh?" Walking over to properly introduce herself.

The subdivision they lived in provided a gate at the front entrance. But none of the homes came with them around the house because the property realtor thought individual fences were tacky. Since the investors provided 24 hour security patrol anyway, they figured the need for them was unnecessary. Although, the residents opposed the decision. None of them ever took the time to complain.

"What's your name?" Cameron asked as she crossed her arms to keep her robe closed, while standing near the edge of his porch. "I'm Cameron and that's my dog Bear." Pointing in her dogs direction who was barking at a squirrel he'd scared up a tree.

"The names Bobby. Nice to meet you." Sizing her up as he thought of a plan for making Tami suffer.

"It's a pleasure meeting you to." Blushing because she thought he was checking her out. "You know you're the first person I've seen in this house since I've moved in. And I've been around the way for a minute now." Trying to engage Bobby in a friendly conversation that would lead to him telling her all of his personal.

"Yeah, my sister saw it on some website that showcases homes for sale. We took the virtual tour of the house and the neighborhood via laptop. After I saw the pictures, I knew she was the one."

"That's convenient."

"I know." He agreed. "I usually don't have the luxury of being able to go out and view homes like normal people, because my job is very demanding. But, I guess I'm one of the lucky ones since I was able to find my home on the web."

"I see… What is it you said you do again?"

"I didn't."

Before he could finish their conversation, they heard a loud bang come from the inside of the house. Bobby immediately jumped to his feet while Cameron tried to see what was going on from whist she stood. Because it was such a disturbing noise, Bear dashed up the stairs and started scratching and barking through the screen. Petrified because he had something to hide, Bobby excused himself and shut the door.

"I didn't know he had company." Frowning as she searched her brain to recall if he mentioned anything about having guests. "That was rude of him." Picking up her pup. "They could have at least come out and introduced themselves." Shaking her head. "Neighbors…" Heading back to her home.

Tami had been up all night plotting on her escape plan. Bobby had left her in the room with no light and little ventilation. Apparently he had time to prep her cage so she thought, because the windows had been covered and both vents were conveniently shut. She wrestled with her thoughts until she gave up relentlessly and decided to go with her instinct of breaking free.

Before Tami could make her get away. She had to be certain her attacker was asleep first. She attempted a calming technique she learned while taking Yoga, which helped her bring her mind and body as one. Placing her mind in a state of meditation, allowed her other senses to elevate. Hearing the birds chirp outside the window let her know it was light out. And the sound of Bobby's voice coming from the other side as well, confirmed he wasn't in the house with her.

Tami's eyelids popped open, while her pupils adjusted to the darkness. She glanced around the room to see if she could see anything that she could use to free herself from the chair, but there was nothing.

"If only I could get my blade out my hair." She whispered as she thought of the three inch razor she used to tie her hair with. A technique she was shown from her mother to make the blade appear to be a fashion clip. "Forget the clip! I'm just stuck." She cried as she hung her head.

Before she engulfed herself in total despair, Tami had one last idea she wanted to try that was bound to work. When the guys tied her to the chair, they only tied her by the wrist. Even though her ankles were bonded to the legs of the seat, her arms weren't. Because her feet rested flat on the floor, she used the muscles in her legs to push her upper body up in an attempt to stand. With her hands tied together, it gave her the right amount of tension to grip the back of the chair with her arms.

Slowly inching her arms up the sides of the chair, Tami's heart was relieved because it sensed her freedom was neigh. Once she managed to loosen up her arms, she realized she was still trapped.

"Okay genus." Shaking her head. "Your hands are still tied together, now what?"

She knew if she could make it to the wall, she could tap the clip on it and it would open. Fall on the floor to pick it up and cut her hands free from behind. Then, loose her feet and she's out. It all sounded like a master plan, but the problem with it was the noise it would create.

Walking over to the wall would be noisy, because the chair would drag behind her. Tapping her head on the wall was a no go, because the thump would be noticeable. And falling on the floor was definitely not an option, because of the bang it would create. Either noise would alert him, which meant she needed the art of surprise on her side in order to escape.

"I guess this is what happens when you don't think a plan all the way through." Easing back down in the chair. "If I wait till he leaves, I'll have a better chance of getting out. Until then, I need to slide my arms back in place." Standing back to her feet. "You know what. Fuck this shit. I'm getting out of here."

Latching both locks; Bobby felt as if he was having a heart attack as he pressed his body up against the door. If anybody found out he was holding someone captive in his home and that the prisoner was a woman. His life would be over in a twinkling of an eye. The police wouldn't care that the prisoner had abducted his sibling first. They'd shoot first and cover up the investigating story later.

Anxiety was no joke and he had enough of those attacks from losing sleep at night. Getting revenge on the person that attacked his sister was important. But, getting caught before he could make her suffer was not on the agenda. Torturing under the radar was the plan and staying off it was even better.

"What the hell was that?" He asked as he looked around both corners of the front room.

At the entrance of Bobby's new home. You would be standing in the living room. Over to the left, you would see a television. A wooden coffee table was placed in front of a gray modular chaise lounge, and behind it would be the bar that separates the kitchen from the living room. To your right you'd see a fish tank, a Bean-bag chair, and a few Lady Palms posted in the corner. Straight ahead was a dark abyss called the hall; which lead to the back end of the residence.

"It's only one thing that could have made a noise as loud as that." Talking to himself as he continued to search the front room for any evidence of something that could have fell. "Tami."

Lying on the floor, Tami's head was throbbing from the impact of her hitting it on the wall and her right arm was hurting from being smashed underneath her body. The plan was genus, but the sacrifice of pulling the job was painful.

"I hope I'm not bleeding." Regrouping as she looked around and noticed the blade close to the door. Sliding across the room in a worm like movement, Tami scooted until she felt the razor touch her fingertips. "Ulrika!" She whispered enthusiastically.

As she sawed at the rope around her wrist, she heard footsteps coming towards her. "Shit!" She mumbled sawing faster. Before she could slit the last thread, the door knob turned. Anxious, she quickly bent the razor and slipped it down the back of her skirt.

"What the fuck!" Bobby yelled as the door hit an unknown object while pushing it open. Because the room was so dark, he couldn't tell what was blocking the entrance, until he flipped the light switch in the hall. "What you doing down there?" He asked. Staring Tami in the eyes as she looked up at him with hers half closed. Because of the brightness of the light, it took her a few seconds longer for her sight to adjust.

"Let me out of here you sick fuck!" Is what she screamed at him. But it sounded different to him because of the tape that was covering her mouth.

"Umm, umm, umm. You say?" He asked as his growing rose from watching her struggle with being bound to the chair. "How does a pretty little thang like you get caught up living the life you're living, huh?" Looking her body over as she continued to fight. "Don't strain yourself. I'll help you up."

Easing in the space between the door opening. Bobby walked around Tami who was still lying in the floor and reached for the string to switch on the light. Bending down to pick her up and place her back in an upright position. He got excited from the sight of her caramel double D breast, which conveniently fell out of her tank top. The dark chocolate Hershey kissed nipple, caught his attention as it perked at the tip of her supple sack from the chill of the room.

Fueled with rage, Tami didn't notice her lady was out greeting the enemy. Until she noticed the sly grin he had plastered on his face. When she looked down to see what he was fixated on. She saw her lefty spewing over and she freaked.

"No, no, no baby doll. Don't cry just yet." He advised. "Wait till you see what I brought for supper first." He laughed. "I guess, since you're all tied up. That means I have to do all the work." Tilting his head side to side as he tried to think of a way to get in without her getting free.

Tami continued to cry while she watched Bobby pace the floor, staring at her like she was a piece of meat.

"Please let me go." She murmured. Hoping he could understand what it was she was trying to say to him.

"You're right." Rubbing his chin. "You can't slob on my knob, because that means I'd have to pull the tape off. If I do that, you may scream." Placing his hands on his hip as he discussed the dilemma with her. "But that's okay. I'll think of something clever." He promised. "I'll be right back, don't you go anywhere." He teased.

Once Tami assumed Bobby would be gone long enough for her to clip the last bit of the knot. She reached down in the back of her skirt in search of her trusty blade. Before she could pull it out, he came back in the room with a knife in his hand. Even if she did manage to cut herself loose. It still wouldn't be quick enough. He'd stab her before she ever got a chance to nab him first.

"Look what I got." Waving the knife childishly in the air. "I figured, hey." Throwing his arm in the air. "If you want the puss. Then dag gone it, you have to work to get it." Bending down to cut the rope tied around her right foot. "Umm, hum." Clearing his throat. "You're about to witness first hand why the ladies call me the cookie monster."

Pulling her body to the edge of the chair, Bobby dragged her panties down her leg until they were trapped between the left and the leg of the seat. He placed his head in the center of her thighs and rested the free one on his right shoulder. The steam from her pussy welcomed him as his face drew closer and closer. Once his lips met the pink thing that was protruding from between her lips, he engulfed it and proceeded to lick and suck until his nose and cheeks were covered with nut. Tami jerked and screamed but nobody heard her. It was tough trying to pull away so he'd stop. But it was even tougher because she was pushing towards him instead.

Bobby continued to devour her as if he hadn't eaten since the last supper. His tongue grooved North, South, East, and West. He slurped until he didn't hear a peep from Tami except the constant splatter noise that came from underneath her skirt.

"You ready now." He said after he wiped his face as he rose off his knees. "For somebody that was fussing like they didn't want the 'D'. She sholl got her gates spread wide open for me to come in." Talking to an unconscious Tami, whose lifeless body was cocked sideways in her chair she was presently occupying, with her legs parted. "Bust it, bust it wide open and I'll tag that putty cat. Bust it, bust it wide open and I'll have her hooked like crack." He sang as he shoved his Mandingo cock in her wet vagina.

Bobby banged in her over and over as if he was in the gym doing cardio. He maneuvered over hurdles. Which were the excess clumps of cum that slide down from her cervix. And he stroked through palpitations her vagina was having, which came from squeezing tightly on his penis every time she had an orgasm. He didn't let up until he was fully drained, hypothetically speaking in regard to his ejaculations.

"What a ride." Falling off her body onto the floor. "Stay golden." He joked. "I need a shower."

Undermining fixing his clothes, Bobby made his way to the bathroom and turned on the shower. Before he stepped in, he turned on the radio and shut the door.

"Ahhh…" He uttered as the water massaged his chest. "That shit was tender." Brushing both hands over his face to toss the water behind his head.

In the other room Tami was defenseless as her body was still lying across the chair. As she slowly opened her eyes, she felt well rested as it seems he fucked her to sleep. Hearing the sound of his voice echoing down the hall singing along with the guy who sang the song Contagious. She struggled to raise her spaghetti body in the upright position, so she could finish what she started.

After cutting herself completely free. Tami picked up the knife Bobby left on the floor and walked toward the bathroom. The plan was to stab him and get away. Instead, she'd soon realize action before thought wasn't a brilliant scheme.

When she reached the door, she slowly propped it open. Apparently, Bobby didn't notice because he continued to sing. She eased her way to the curtain and before she could reach in, Bobby reached out and grabbed her. What she didn't know is he saw the door open as he turned to rinse the soap from underneath his arm. Tami was caught by surprise, but she was able to cut him on the side of his forehead as he had her in a head lock.

"You came back for more, huh?" Slamming her left hand against the wall to knock the knife out of her grip as he continued to choke.

He walked her over to the sink and bent her over. Using his arm to bend hers behind her back. He let go of the grip he had around her neck to shove his penis in her ass.

"Ahhh!!!" She screamed as her muscle reflex caused her body to stand up straight.

"Yeah bitch!" Running his right hand up the front of her body until he reached her throat. "Take this dick!"

Bobby bent her arm and choked as he shoved his wood up the spine of her back. He didn't let up because of her screams and he continued to jam until her screams turned to squeals.

"You thought you caught me slipping, didn't you?" Thrusting in her hole. "It hurts now, but I'm about to nut. That will sooth the sting, but I ain't clocking out just yet."

Tami felt a instant warmth on the inside of her line. Now that his tug was more with ease. It signified to her he had released his pressure.

"Give me that pussy!" He demanded pulling out her ass. Twisting her around on her back. Throwing her body against the sink.

"Fuck me." She whispered. Using her hands to spread her pussy lips to invite him in.

Confused by the sudden willingness to corporate with what was supposed to be a robbery. Bobby wrapped his arms around her body and hid his body part in her doll house. They fucked one another on that counter until his dick refused to rise again.

Walking back onto her property, Cameron greeted another neighbor of hers, who had stepped out to retrieve her mail as well. Standing in the middle of her driveway. Cameron continued to hold tight to Bear who was tugging on her sleeve, while she conversed. Aggravated by his constant movement, she freed him and laughed as he rolled around on his back in the grass playfully.

"You're right. I was just saying the same thing to Bobby a few minutes ago." She agreed. "It is nice out here today." Crossing her arms to make sure her robe remained closed. "Thank you for the soup the other day! I really appreciated it!" She yelled. "You have to give me the recipe one of these days." Laughing as she walked up the stairs. "I'll check you later Mrs. Hattie! Thank you again!"

Now that the weekend had arrived, Cameron had planned to hang out with her number one girl and end her night with a shot of vodka and a sip of lime. Because they had gotten their nails done earlier that week, she set up a hair appointment for 3:00 p.m. and is supposed to rendezvous with Step after.

"I need to pick up the pace a little bit. I am not trying to hear Lauren's mouth about being late." Grabbing her wash cloth from off the rack as she prepped her water.

While rinsing the suds off of her caramel skin, Cameron imagined what it would be like if Dexter was there showering with her. She pictured him slowly moving his loofa up her back as he teased her rear cheeks with the touch of his ego. If he was there; he'd wrap his arms around her body from behind and tickle the point of her breast with his finger tips. Forcing the bubbles to rotate around her nipple like a merry go round. As both bodies glide against each other. They would wash clean from the lather they would create. Easy access with a steamy ending, satisfaction guaranteed.

Startled by the barking of her pup. Cameron rushed through her last wash and hopped out the shower. "That dog is going to be the death of me." She whined.

SNOOPING AROUND

Merging off the interstate. Cameron dashed into the flow of traffic without using her turn signal. One of the drivers behind her got angry and blew his horn at her, while another sped past and flipped her off. Cameron paid neither of them any mind. She knew if she didn't get to 'Slick Ends' hair salon in the next twelve minutes. Lauren would take another guest and she'd have to wait.

Parking in one of the vacant spaces in front of 'Rod's Gym'. Cameron sprung out of her vehicle and sprinted to the door.

"I see you got here on time." Laughing as she watched her client struggle to catch her next breath.

"Damn right!" Wiping the sweat from her forehead. "I have some things I need to get done today. I can't be stuck up in here all morning over one minute." Flopping down on the stool.

"Well, time is money. And I don't have enough of either to waist." Lauren stated as she swung one of her capes around Cameron's shoulders to protect her clothing from hair strands. "Every minute lost, is another dollar missed."

"Yeah, yeah…"

"So, what look are you going for this time?" Spinning the stool around so her client could view herself in the mirror.

"Cut me."

"What!" Hoping Cameron was joking about cutting her hair.

"I want to try something new." Turning her head side to side as she pictured herself with a bob or a pixie cut. "I'd be twenty-eight in October and I want to do something different."

"I hear what you're saying, but I'm ignoring the foolishness that's coming out at the same time. You got all of this good hair, not to mention it's healthy as well. And you just want to whack it all off." Resting her hands on her hips. "Women now-a-days." Shaking her head. "Always taking action before they think some of their decisions all the way through." Wrapping a towel around Cameron's neck. "It's your hair and your money. If that's what you want to do, then who am I to stop you." Using her right foot to pump the lever connected to the back of the chair. "How short do you want to go?"

"Pixie, real low."

"Pixie!" Shocked by the sudden jump from long to pixie.

"Yeah, you don't think it will be cute on me?"

"Cute or not. The maintenance is what you need to be worrying about. But, go ahead and do you. I'm here for you whenever you need a fixing." Grinning deviously. "Come on so I can get started on your wash." Walking over to the sink.

Cameron understood what Lauren was trying to tell her, but she had already made up in her mind she was going to follow through with the change. For twenty-seven years of her life she had been rocking the same look. Even if she changed the style occasionally. She still felt she looked the same. It was time for her to release some old baggage and turn over a new leaf. And getting rid of the hair was first on the 'to-do list'.

After sitting for two and a half hours, Lauren was finally finished with Cameron's new do. Using her fingers to spread some of the curls out, Lauren spun the chair around and revealed her creation to her client.

"Wahl ah!!!"

Cameron was speechless. She couldn't believe the image she saw staring back at her. This was it. This woman was her. If she'd known she'd look this good with short hair years ago. She would've been cut it off.

"Wow…"

"I know right. I said the same thing, but I didn't want to ruin it for you."

"You did your thing with this one honey." Using her hand mirror for its reflection to view the back of her head.

"Well, you know. I do what I can, when I can." Pulling the cape off Cameron's shoulders. "Now hand me my money and move. I got someone else waiting to be seen." She demanded.

"I can't even be mad at you right now." Still looking in the mirror. "You hooked me up."

"Exactly, now tell a friend and get out the way."

"Thanks again Lauren. You really have made my day with this." Counting out sixty-five dollars.

"I'm glad you like it. Remember, if you don't have a half wrap scarf. Just wrap your hair in a clock wise direction before you tie it down."

"Gotcha." Raising out of the seat. "See you in another two weeks."

After meeting Stephanie at the mall and shopping till they dropped. The girls were tired and ready to part ways. Because Rico was due to come home in a couple days. Stephanie wanted to be alone again before he arrived. She knew when he did come. They would make up for lost time.

Therefore she didn't invite Cameron over and she knew Cam didn't let people sleep over unless they were leaving before the neighbors woke.

"I've been ripping and running all day." Rubbing her aching stomach. "I think I'll treat myself to a nice quiet dinner." Pulling into a fancy steak house nearby. "Dinner for one is always exquisite, because you can eat whatever and however you want, without having to eat salads or watch your manners."

When her table was ready. The waitress came over and escorted her to be seated. "Your waiter will be with you shortly. Would you care for something to drink while you wait?"

"Yes, a water please."

"Sure thing." Placing a menu on the table. "Here's a menu for you to look over while you wait. And your server will be here shortly with your drink."

"Thank you." Smiling as she nodded her head.

"My pleasure."

While Cameron sat patiently for her waiter to come, she scanned the room and gazed at the people as they dined and talked. Valentine's Day was three weeks away and this was the first time in years she'd ever been bothered about not having someone special. Sure she had Dexter and Albert. But, neither one of them was hers. They both brought her gifts, but one would have it shipped to be delivered on that day. And the other would come by with his on the 15th. Being single had its advantages, but the disadvantages weighed heavy on the heart when you have too much time to think.

"Excuse me." Distracted by the waiter. "My name is Reese and I will be your server for the evening." Pulling his note pad out of his apron to prepare to take her order.

"Hey, I know you." She blushed. "You're that guy from Lashay's."

Standing her menu in an upright position.

"Yes, I work there. But, I don't recall ever meeting you ma'am." Sitting a straw next to her cup.

"I saw you the other night when I was there visiting Stephanie."

"Oh yeah, I remember you now. Did you do something different? I thought your hair was much longer if I'm not mistaken."

"It actually was" she giggled. "I had it cut earlier today." Feeling overwhelmed because she didn't expect to see him there. And impressed because he had not one but two jobs.

"Okay." Placing napkins down on the table. "Would you like me to come back to take your order when your dinner guest have arrived?"

"That won't be necessary. I'm dinning alone this evening." Embarrassed because she didn't have anyone to dine with.

"Really?" Shocked for he didn't understand how a beautiful woman like Cameron could be having dinner by herself. Unescorted by a guy friend or even a best friend. "Are you seeing anyone?"

"Noooo." Holding her head down. "Not at the moment." Gazing back up at Reese who had a confused look on his face.

"Good, because dinners on me." Placing a second set of silverware down on the table.

"Wow." Stunned by his take charge demeanor. "Thank you."

"Don't mention it." Slinging his dish cloth over his right shoulder. "I'll take my break now, just so I can sit here and get to know more about you."

"Really." Sizing him up. *Look at him. Trying to play a man's game with his young self. He wouldn't know what to do with a woman like me, even if I did give him the opportunity to entertain.*

Cameron was already aware of him being two years younger than she, and she knew he had a daughter as well. What more info could he share that would cause her to continue to look at him as eye candy and not dating material. To her the only thing he had to offer or bring to the table per say was sex. And she gets enough of that from the men she's rotating back and forth now.

Taking him serious was out the question, because he was too young to have a real adult relationship. She felt giving him an ounce of hope that something would come out of this dinner. Would be a waste of both their time. #1 because he was still in the game playing stage and #2 she didn't have time for any child's play.

After having been gone for twenty minute, Reese returned to the table with two plates, one for him and the other for her. Apparently, he'd taken it upon himself to decide what it was she was going to eat, instead of letting her choose. Astonished by his choice, Cameron welcomed him openly to a nice yet friendly conversation. But little did he know she was the one he should beware of.

"So, tell me." Picking up her utensils. "What's on your mind?" She asked as she cut into her T-bone.

"I'm just wondering how can a woman such as yourself. Be left alone to fin for herself." Washing down a spoonful of mashed potatoes with a glass of wine. "I figure either it's something wrong with you, or it's something wrong with the men you choose to date." Staring her directly in her eyes.

"Of course we both know I'm going to say there's nothing wrong with me, but I digress." Grabbing her cup.

"So, what is it then?" Placing both hands on the table. "Have your sugar turned into spice?"

As a mouthful of water came spewing out of Cameron's mouth, she couldn't believe some of the things this young man was saying to her. Here sat a twenty-five year old boy with titty milk still on his breath, asking a grown woman if her pussy juice sour. The nerve of this jerk she thought.

"My sugar cane fluids are still sweet, if you must know." Pressing her napkin against her lips to dry them.

"When you're ready to test that theory. You know where to find me." Excusing himself from the table. "You never know. I may discover flavors you never knew you had. Pardon me, I meant to say could create." Picking up his place setting from which he sat.

Cameron couldn't believe it. His arrogance and his confidence was way over the top. She had never been spoken to in such a manner by anyone past or present. It was unnerving the way he made her feel. It had been said that birds of a feather flop together. By them having the same opinions regarding relationships from past experiences. Reese knew he could push a few buttons when speaking to her. But it never crossed his mind that Cameron had feelings as well. Yet he hurt them anyway.

Pulling in the driveway, Cameron noticed Bobby's house was pitch black on the inside and out. Not one light was on and he had forgotten to turn his porch light on also. She figured he was home because his car was still parked on the lawn. Then again, he could have left with the hoodlums she saw over at his place the other day. As she got out of her vehicle, she reached back in to grab her hodo. In doing so; she heard what sounded like a woman scream coming from the back of her neighbor's home. Startled, she quietly closed the door and waited to set the alarm. Remembering the incident from the other night, she tip toed across their adjoining lawns to get a closer view of what could be going on.

As she approached the side panel, Cameron noticed a red light flashing on and off through one of the back windows. Fully aware of it being illegal to trespass on someone else's property. She ignored her intuitional warning and proceeded back to her home. After placing her foot on the porch, Bobby came bursting out the front door onto his patio. Spooked, she jumped and turned to greet him.

"Hey there." Waving her arm back and forth in the air, but Bobby never said a word. He just stood in the center and lite his cigarette. Nodding his head at her as the smoke he exhaled entered the atmosphere. "Is everything alright?" She asked. "I heard a scream a few minutes ago as I was getting out the car and I got concerned." Waiting on him to respond. "Well, you know if you need anything. I'm just a few steps away." She assured him. But Bobby continued to stare and puff.

The creepiness of their current situation sent chills up her spine. Therefore she hurried herself in the house.

"That was close." Holding tightly to the door handle. "If I didn't come away from back there when I did. He would have caught me." Rushing over to the nearest window to see what she could see. "What the heck is going on over there?" She questioned herself as she peered out the blinds. "I know that scream came from his place. I'm sure of it." To her surprise, Bobby was looking directly at her. Even though it was indeed dark out. She was certain he was because the fire from his cigarette was pointing in her direction. "Oh shit!" She shouted as she pulled away from the glass. "Please, please, please don't let him come over here. I don't know nothing and I most defiantly haven't seen anything." She welled frantically. "If I can make it through the night. I'll make something shake for tomorrow."

Tami and Bobby had been coupe up in the house the entire day. Even though Tami had shown Bobby she was down for the sexual activities he forced on her. He still didn't trust her. When the morning had come, he tied her back to the chair and started breakfast. Knowing the time was nearing when he would have to deal with her for taking his sister. Bobby couldn't help how amazing the past several days had been with her being there.

While sitting back in the place she had started from in the beginning of her escape. Tami scoped the room around once more for the sake of trying and saw nothing useful to help her break free. With all odds against her, she still had no intention of giving up hope.

"I made us the original." Placing both plates on the floor. "Here you have your cheese grits, eggs, smoked hickory bacon, toast, and grape jelly on the side as spread." Smiling while making a few uneasy grunting noises. "Now, I'm going to pull the tape from your mouth. Only if you promise me you'll behave." Bending down to face her directly. "Play nice, you live. Get crazy, you die. Kapish." Awaiting her nod. "Okay."

In the mist of Bobby feeding Tami and eating himself, he received a phone call. Because he didn't want to risk answering it in front of her, he excused himself from the room and stepped outside.

"What's good?"

"What's the plan for dumping the package?" Paul asked.

"Right now...." Before he was able to finish his statement a loud scream came from the inside of the house. Bobby panicked. All it took was for one person, just one. To find out she was tied up in there and his life would be over.

Tami screamed and she yelled to the top of her lungs for someone to come to her rescue. Because Bobby failed to tape her lips back shut. She felt this was her only opportunity to get noticed. It didn't matter to her one way or the other if that person was a kid or an adult. Just as long as someone knew she was there.

Storming back in, Bobby ran down the hall and shut the bedroom door behind him, leaving the main entrance wide open.

"You want to scream?" He shouted. "I'd give you a reason to scream!"

He slapped and punched her in the face until her eyes and lips were swollen and red. Once he had beaten her senseless, he slammed her on the floor and raped her repeatedly. It didn't faze him not once that she was choking on her own blood. He continued in rage. Tami was so bruised up, that if someone came in and saw her that knew her personally. Wouldn't recognize her from the way she looked at that moment.

"That ought to have taught you a lesson." Walking out of the room as he adjusted his pants, covered in blood and sweat. As he took his time walking back up the hall to close the door. He noticed Bear standing at his screen barking directly at him. While approaching, he saw a shadow cross his window and that's when he stood face to face with Cameron. Neither of them said a thing. She grabbed her dog and scurried back to her place.

Thinking she had been living in a nightmare. Cameron didn't know what else she could do. In the beginning she tried to tell her best friend something strange was going on with Bobby the first day he moved in. She didn't know what exactly, but she knew it was something fishy about him. Going to the police would be a waste of time because she didn't have any evidence to present to them of him doing something foul. Which meant she had to do some investigating of her own in order to nail him.

"He thinks he nickel slick, but I got his penny change." She said as she walked back to her door step. "I caught him this time. Doing what, I don't know. But, time will reveal everything I need to see eventually." Rambling threw her attire she had hanging in her bedroom closet. "Let me get myself together. He ain't about to ruin my weekend."

Albert had text Cameron late last night and stated he wanted to take her to brunch and spend the afternoon with her on the town. Cameron knew by Albert making it clear he would be available to her. She wasn't going to miss the opportunity to talk him into replacing all four of her tires. It was time for her vehicles annual inspection and if she could convince him to take some of the load off her shoulders. She'd have extra money to go out of town.

"Hey sweetie," she greeted as she sashayed over to Albert's Range. "Did you miss me?"

"You're always missed when you're not around."

"Is that right?" Puckering her lips. If it was someone else she wouldn't have believed them. But she knew he was being honest with her, because he always take the initiative to call and check in.

"Of course, who wouldn't miss a set of lips as those." Wrapping his arms around her waist to lift her up.

"Woah!" She giggled. "Looks like someone's been working out."

"Naa... Just excited to see you, is all." Blushing as he continued to squeeze on her.

"I need a favor mac daddy."

"And..."

"Could you replace my tires for me today?" Hanging tight to his neck.

"That's all?" He puckered. "I thought you were going to ask me for a new car or something."

"Should I?" Wanting to see where her limit lies.

"Ha, ha sweet cake. Let's start with the tires first."

Albert was a regular Joe, but he was a phenomenal saver. He didn't have a lot, but his cheap ways made it easy for him to spoil his lady. Cameron knew Albert was a cheap skate. But she also knew if she mentioned she needed something done that was of great importance, he would take care of it no questions asked. Which ran in her favor every time. It may have been wrong what she was doing, but she thought otherwise. She figured as much time he spent away from her and doing whatever else he felt was important than giving her his full attention. He could make up for it by turning his pockets inside out.

RAIN ON ME

Arnez had been on a drunken rampage since the death of his girlfriend. A year had flown by and the closer it gets to Jasmine's burial date. The more alcohol he consumes. The club was still bringing in a nice portion of revenue for him, which had made up for the drop in sales from Stylez. Even though he was still on cloud nine financially, he felt as if he was walking through hell emotionally. Because the 'Spot' bring back so many memories, he decided to part ways with it.

Letting the phone continue to go to the answering machine, Arnez just laid there with his arm across his face to shield his puffy eyes from the sunlight. He had made up in his mind that he was going to take another week off and lay around until he heard Shelly leaving a message on the machine.

"Hey Arnez, it's Shelly. Just calling to see how things have been going for you lately. I heard you were in the process of selling the club." Before she could finish leaving her message, he picked up.

"Hey Shell."

"Hey!" She greeted him enthusiastically. "Why you sound like your breath stank?" She giggled.

"Hell, it might do." He laughed as he did a quick breath check. "What's going on?"

"Nothing really, just calling to check in on you." Wiping the tears from her eyes. "I heard you were selling the club."

"Yeah…" Letting out a deep breath. "I've had a few meetings with a couple of possible buyers that's interested in taking over."

"I know I haven't been there since the incident, but why the sudden need to sell?"

"Honestly, I haven't been there either." Sitting up in his bed. "Ever since I've lost Jazz. The place ain't felt the same to me." Sliding his hand over his face. "Almost as if my memories of her are haunting me, whenever I step foot in that place."

"I know what you mean. But you have to move on it's been a year Arnez. You can't harbor on those feelings forever or you'd miss out on the biggest blessing you have."

"And what's that?"

"Life."

"I hear what you're saying. Trust me I do, but I'm still going to sell. Get out while I still can, you know."

Little did Shelly know, Arnez had a secret he had been keeping from his past. His sister had gotten herself in some big trouble and he had to pull all his resources to get enough money to bail her out. Two months before the day, he received a certified letter in the mail from his sister Tami. Stating she was about to make a business play that could potentially get her in a bind. If he didn't hear from her in a full week time frame, that meant something went wrong.

Because of the lifestyle she chose to live, they made plans years prior to only communicate through certified mail. And if shit ever hit the fan, pack up and head for the border. Arnez never thought the day would come when he would have to make good on that promise. But as fate may have it, shit was getting realer by the day. The week had come and gone and there wasn't a letter from Tam. Whether he liked it or not, he had to do what needed to be done.

"Why you talking like somebody after you or something?"

"It's not that. I haven't heard from my sister in a week and I'm starting to get a little concerned about her. That's all." Adjusting his boxers as he headed towards the bathroom adjacent to his room.

"I didn't know you had a sister." Suddenly vested in what else he could have been keeping secret from her. "I thought I knew all there was to know about Mr. Arnez Jenkins." Using sarcasm to manipulate him into telling her more about his personal. "I know there's a thin line between business and personal, but I thought we were close enough for me to know you had a sibling." Trying to make him feel guilty.

"Yeah, I don't talk about her much." Opening the medicine cabinet.

"I see."

"We both are entrepreneurs, but we have different philosophies regarding making money." Smearing toothpaste on his blue electronic tooth brush.

"How so?"

"How about we save that conversation for another day." Shoving the brush in his mouth. "I'll call you later this afternoon to let you know how the sell went. Maybe then we can make some time to go over some new ideas concerning 'Shine'." Mumbling under the loud buzzing as he brushed.

"Sounds like a plan." Shelly agreed. "We'll chat later."

"Alright."

"Bye." Hanging up the phone.

After brushing his teeth. Arnez went to check his porch one last time to see if the postman left a package from his sister. But as he looked around, there wasn't one. In that moment he knew it was time to go.

Pulling into the parking lot, Arnez noticed a white Suburban parked by the entrance. He knew it couldn't have been the carpet cleaners, because they usually come between 6a.m. and 8a.m, before the crew get in to set up. Usually Rock is there early but Arnez didn't see his Crown Vick parked anywhere.

"I wonder if this is another buyer wanting to check the place out." Placing his Lamborghini in park. Arnez hopped out to greet his guest, but before he could shake his hand. Two more guys jumped out the truck and surrounded him by the door.

"Are you the cat that own this joint?" Turk asked with a straw hanging out the right side of his mouth.

"Yeah, I own the place." He responded with his chin up and his chest out. No matter what the circumstance maybe or how outnumbered he was. Arnez wasn't going to back down. His mother didn't raise no wimp. "What's it to you?"

"Ha, ha…" Turk laughed. "This nigga surrounded and he still got heart. I can respect it." Taking the straw from his mouth. "But this ain't no sack check fool. Brace yourself!" He shouted.

In that moment Arnez received one of the worst beatings he'd ever received in his life. And the sad part about it is the fact that he was just an innocent bystander, stuck in the middle of his sisters drama. Blow after blow; the boys pounded on Arnez as if they were in a batting cage, practicing for the major leagues championship game. When Rock finally pulled up three hours later he saw Arnez's car, but he noticed the bolt lock was still on the door.

"That's odd." Parking by the valet ropes. "Nez must've dropped his car off and rode with someone else." Using his automatic lock pad to secure his vehicle.

As he neared the midnight blue foreign. Rock noticed an overturned cognac loafer next to the rear passenger tire. "Is that a shoe?" Walking over to pick it up. While approaching to retrieve it, he then saw Arnez lying in a pool of blood beaten so badly that the white meat was revealed on his left shoulder.

"Damn homes!" He shouted as he kneeled down to check for a pulse. "What in the hell done happened to you?" Still talking while he felt for a pulse on the side of Arnez's neck. "Hang tight my dude, help is on the way." Dialing for the authorities.

When Shelly stepped into the holding room at Greenstone Hospital, she couldn't believe her eyes. Arnez was hooked up to a breathing machine and had an IV shoved in his arm for nutrition. The feeling she felt when she saw him in his current state, brought back emotions she knew oh to well.

"Damn…" Michael mumbled as he placed his arm around her.

"I can't believe this!" She wells. "First Nette gets into an accident. Then Jazz commits suicide, and now this!" Crying in his chest. "What now?" She asks rhetorically. "What am I supposed to do? I can't stand to lose another friend. Not right now and not like this." Walking over to the bed her friend was currently occupying. "What happened to you? Who did this to you?" Rubbing her hand across his forehead. "What have you gotten yourself into??" Taking a deep breath as she tried to hold back the snot that was rolling off the edge of her nostrils. "All I'm asking is that you don't leave me. Not now, I can't handle another loss."

"Shell…" He muzzled under his voice.

"Arnez!" Shelly shouted, slamming her fist down in his chest.

"Ughh," he yelled.

"Sorry, sorry, sorry." She pleaded as she wrapped her hands around his. "What happened? We'd talked just a few hours ago. What's going on?"

"They…" He coughs. "They got Tami."

"Who got Tami?" Confused because she doesn't know the lady he's talking about. "Who is Tami?"

"My sister!" He coughs repeatedly. This time as a result from choking on his own spit. "They said." Attempting to sit up in the bed.

"Don't try to move, just lay down. I can understand what you're saying." Helping him get back in a comfortable position. "Don't strain yourself."

"They said if I don't give them $700,000 dollars this time come Monday. She's dead." Wheezing as he inhaled the artificial oxygen from his breathing tube. "I have the money, but I don't know where the drop off is."

"Really…" Shocked by the news. "What is it that your sister does exactly?" All ears while she awaits his answer as to why someone would want to kidnap his sister.

"She's a dealer."

"A car dealer?" Michael butted in.

"A drug dealer." He replies as he rests his head on the cool pillow with his eyes shut. "I know she told me if anything like this ever happened, to leave the country and forget about her. But, I can't Shell." Feeling guilty for not being there for her in her most vulnerable time of need. "She's my only sibling. I have to try and save her. I couldn't live with myself if I didn't try."

"I know what you mean, but look at you." Pointing out the obvious. "What can you do? You can't even walk straight, let alone defend yourself." Hoping he'd be more rational about the decision he chooses to make. She'd never tell him to forget about saving her, she just wants him to consider going to the authorities instead.

"True enough, but I have to try." Gripping her hand tightly. "You know I wouldn't do anything to put you in harms way, right?"

"Yeah, I know."

"But, I could really use your help right about now."

"I don't know Arnez." Wondering what it is he was about to ask her to do. "If I'm going to end up like you in the end. Then, I can't help you."

"You won't." He guarantees. "I promise you, you'll be safe."

"How can you be so sure?"

"My cousin works with the Feds and he's going to be with you every step of the way. I asked Rock to give him a call before he left to let him know what's going on and I needed him to come through." Massaging the pain in his left arm. "You won't be alone." He assures her. "We could use your help as well."

"For sure. Anything you need." He agrees without any second guessing his decision. "Loyalty has no ends with me. I got you."

"Thanks."

Even though Shelly wanted to help Arnez save his sister. Something didn't sit right with her about doing so. When she first started out with her dream of becoming a designer. No one really believed in her, not even her own family. All she had was Kelly, until she was introduced to Arnez. And in a blink of an eye, he changed her life forever. It was as if R. Kelly was in the background singing 'did you ever think that you'd be this rich'. She owed him everything.

Not only did he date her best friend, but Arnez became a part of their adoptive family. Within a short period of time. She couldn't turn her back on him in his hour of need. He made her a promise that she'd be safe and with his cousin being the law. Whatever they had planned for her couldn't be that risky. Especially with them knowing she practically had a toddler at home awaiting her return. Wanting to go with her gut, she decided to say yes. Jasmine would have appreciated it.

"I'm in."

Things were starting to get a bit more complicated than expected. Bobby didn't have the slightest idea of what his next move should be. Tami had been getting the better part of his emotions lately and Cameron continued to snoop around his house like the nosey neighbor she was. He needed a plan to move his hostage to another location, but he couldn't do it with Cameron creeping around. Bobby could sense something huge was coming, but he didn't want to get caught in the cross fires when it all goes down.

"We have a problem." Using a mellow tone so Tami couldn't overhear his conversation. "Where are you guys?"

"Just got through tying up some loose ends. What's going on?"

"Start making a beeline over this way. We need to come up with a solution to this problem asap."

"We on the way."

After hanging up with Paul, Bobby pulled out one of the stools from underneath his bar and took a seat. Reminiscing on the events that took place earlier that week, he began questioning himself if he made the right decision by retaliating on Tami for taking Mo. Even if he wanted to make things right between them two. He felt he was already knee deep in this sink hole Tami had created for the both of them.

Standing in the kitchen, Paul was leaning up against the wall as he slow dragged on his Newport. Bobby was still hunched over on the bar, while Murf rolled a blunt on the couch and Turk paced the living room floor.

"What's the plan?"

"Pull yourself together man, damn!" Paul shouted as he watched his best friend fall apart before his eyes. "Out of all the years we've known each other. I ain't never seen you act as sensitive as you've been acting around here lately." Pointing his cigarette in his direction.

Bobby may have been the brains of the operation and all other endeavors these guys chose to indulge themselves in. But everyone can clearly see that Paul was the spine.

"We messed dude up!" Turk bragged. "Never in a million years would he have ever seen that butt whooping coming." Using his boxing techniques to reenact their encounter with Arnez.

"Yeah…" Murf agreed. "Dude was jacked up." Chuckling as he licked the rello wrap he was folding. "I wonder if he survived that shit."

"Man, that nigga still alive."

"He better had pulled through if we plan on getting that money!" Paul butted in angrily.

"What money?" Naïve to what the fellas was talking about.

"The ransom money." Turk informed as he continued to bounce around as if he was floating like a butterfly.

"You mean to tell me y'all ran up on shorty brother!" Jumping off the stool in rage. Furious because he didn't expect for things to go as far as to request a ransom.

"Yeah, what else were we going to do?" Now standing Bobby face to face.

"I don't know!" Placing both hands on his head. "Anything but that!"

"Look, the way I see it. We didn't have no other choice." Leaning back up against the wall. "If we let her walk scott free without getting paid, she'd retaliate or snitch. If we killed her without getting the doe. We'd have a dead body to cover up and be out $700,000. Possibly facing jail time once the body is found and we all know them bastards are going to find the body. The only way I see us getting away is if we wear plastic over our shoes, clothes, hands, and hair nets."

"Toss her with the gators!" Murf added jokingly. "The perfect murder."

"I say toss her with the fishes, because the alligators never finish the job." Walking over to share the blunt with his twin.

"Parana's don't' sound like a bad idea."

"How the hell do y'all plan on transporting a dead body out the country? Let alone across the border and state line, without getting flagged by customs?" Paul asked as he awaited his genus friends to fill him in on the plot they all seem to agree upon.

"Shit, I don't know!" Bobby chuckled. "I was just going along with what everybody else was suggesting."

"I need you to think! You supposed to be the smart one and here you are throwing out foolish proposals and making light of our situation and I don't see nothing funny about what we got going on."

"I've been having these dreams lately about past shit that happened back in the hood." He admitted. "I feel like something big is about to go down, but I don't know what." Getting a nervous chill. "Shit has been getting hot. Especially with that neighbor of mine that keep popping up at my door step every time I turn around."

Everyone knew who Cameron was. They remembered catching her looking at them one afternoon they were standing in the yard discussing Mo. Neither of them would have guess she'd become a problem for them, but she has. But, if she needed to be erased. Then that was something neither of them would hesitate on doing.

"You're just overthinking things right now. Which is understandable. But you need to suck it up and let's move forward on taking care of what we need to take care of and deal with our past demons later." Paul advise.

"Alright man."

COOKIES ANYONE

Saturday had finally come and gone and Cameron planned on staying in bed all day today, hopefully with no interruptions. Normally she'd spend her Sunday mornings in church, but since she had a fun filled evening entertaining her boo daddy. She figured missing one Sunday wouldn't hurt to bad.

"Umm... I had a good time last night." Smiling at Bear as he gave her the 'pity' look. "Are you even listening to me?" She asked her pup who was clearly ignoring her. "Some best friend you are." Pushing him off the bed. "Ugghh..." Stretching her body underneath the covers. "I wonder what Step got going for today?" Reaching for her cellular phone. "Naa... That's alright. I'm going to." She sings. "Just chill." Serenading in her best soprano voice she could belch out while laying down. "I wonder what that crazy neighbor of mine is up to." Turning towards her window. "He's always acting suspicious with his weird ass." Rubbing her feet together to stir up some heat. "Why he had to move next to me?"

Suddenly, Cameron gets a phone call from Stephanie. After deciding she was going to spend some alone time with herself, she ignored the call. Immediately after the phone stopped ringing, she received a text.

"Ugh…" She grunted. "I know it ain't nobody but Step!"

Scrolling threw her messages. She came across one that was titled 'emergency'. "Of course it is."

Stephanie: I know you saw me calling you trick! Anyway, you remember my friend Antoinette that works for her sister Shelly at that boutique we went to the other day? Well bitch, she said she's on a stake out. Guess where bitch. At your neighbor's house!

"What!" Cameron shouts as she leaps out of bed. "What the hell!" Peering out the corner of her blinds. "What the heck is going on around here?" Spotting Shelly walking up to Bobby's door with a box of girl scout cookies in her hand. "I didn't know she knew him." Watching her draw closer to his door. "Something fishy is going on around here, and I knew something was wrong with that bastard when I first laid eyes on him."

Inhale, exhale. Inhale, exhale is all Shelly concentrated on as she approached the door. Sweating bullets because she was afraid if she didn't stick to the script, her life could be in jeopardy. Carrying a box filled with docey-dos and tagalongs didn't make her feel any secure with the disguise. But Arnez cousin felt a beautiful young mother going door to door selling cookies was a good get up. No straight man in his right mind could turn down that cookie and a smile.

Now facing Bobby's door. The moment of truth had arrived. Each box was tagged with an invisible bug that looked like a scratch and sniff sticker. Therefore, no matter which box he chose. They'd have ears on the inside. All Shelly have to do now is push the doorbell.

"Who is it?" A startled Bobby yelled. *It better not be that damn neighbor of mine or she gon' get what's coming to her.*

Because Tami stayed awake the entire night trying to figure out a way to make an escape. She heard the bell when it sounded as well.

"Fuck!" He shouted. "I hope this bitch don't try nothing when I answer this door. I'd hate to have to add another body to the playing field." Sliding his g-lock down the back of his pants.

Before Bobby went to answer the door, he stuck his head in the room Tami was in to give her a little piece of advice. "Don't try nothing bitch." He whispered. Since she had tape over her mouth. She had to nod her head in agreement to acknowledge his warning. As Shelly reached to push the bell one last time. Bobby opened the door before she could press it.

"Good morning." She greeted with a welcoming smile on her face.

"Yeah," he replied. Scoping the neighborhood out above her head to make sure no one was outside. Especially that nosey neighbor of his. But, unbeknownst to him. She was already posted in her bedroom window. Ready to witness whatever was about to jump off.

"Would you care to purchase a box of girl scout cookies?" Smiling as she pulled a carton from the box. "I only have two flavors with me here. But, if you'd like something different. It won't be no trouble for me to grab it out my car for you."

"What kind do you have?"

"Right now I have docey-dos and tagalongs."

"How much are you selling them for?"

"They're three dollars and fifty-cents a box."

"I thought little girls sale girl scout cookies, not adults." Raising his left brow.

"Normally they do, but my daughter is sick right now and we still have a deadline to meet." She giggled.

"I see…" Noticing Shelly's smile was beginning to fade away. "Riddle me this."

"Okay."

"Where's your car?" Sliding his right hand behind his back.

"Ohh!" She laughed. "Way down there." Pointing at a black Ford Taurus parked four houses down.

Because of the wires on the cookies. The agents that were staking out in the Taurus was able to duck down before they had a chance to be spotted.

"I was moving door to door on foot and forgot all about having drove my vehicle." She giggled. "Silly rabbit."

"Umm hum…" Feeling as if something was off about this cookie pusher. "Give me three boxes of the tagalongs and that'll do it for me."

As Shelly reached in the box, she heard a loud bang come from the inside of Bobby's house. Startled by the noise. She looked up, but didn't expect to be staring down the barrel of another gun.

"Hand over the cookies and back the fuck back." Stating in an assertive tone.

"Ahh shit!" Cameron sang as she watched from a far. "She finna get it now."

Doing as she was told. Shelly handed over the cookies without getting paid and scurried back down the driveway.

"Please don't shoot. Please don't shoot." She cried to herself as she inched her way down the street. Once she was in clear view of the Taurus, she dropped the box and ran for the door.

"What the heck was that!" She argued.

"Breath, just breath." One of the agents advised as he conducted a breathing exercise to try and calm her down.

"Where the fuck was y'all and Captain Save a Ho, when he pulled that gun out on me?" Too angry to wipe the sweat from her face. "What were y'all waiting for? You could've grabbed him then!" She nagged.

"He didn't do anything wrong." Terrance replied.

"What you mean?" Appalled by his insensitive response. "That nigga put a gun to my head over some fucking cookies! And you going to sit there and say he didn't do anything wrong!" Ready to slap the taste out Arnez's cousin mouth. "If he would've blown my brains out, then what Terrance?"

"He didn't!" The accompanying agent replied.

"Look Shell, if we would've moved in on him at that moment. Our cover would've been blown and that innocent woman trapped in that house. Could have lost her life over one rookie mistake, and you could have to. If that would have happened, this whole operation would have been compromised and months of investigation would have been flushed down the drain. We've spent years trying to bust this guy on something solid and now that we have a lead. We're not trying to lose it. Do you want that to happen?"

"No."

"Okay then. You have to trust my judgment and know we have everything under control." He reassures her. "Our team did a behavior analysis test on the on-sub and he isn't the murdering in cold blood type of guy. Something had to trigger him to behave in such a manner as this to kidnap our victim." He explains. "If he wanted you dead, you wouldn't be sitting here right now. You understand?"

"Yes, I understand. And please don't talk to me like I'm remedial." Moving her shirt back and forth to allow some air to circulate throughout.

"Good work out there!" Terrance congratulated her. "Because of your bravery, we now have confirmation that Tami is indeed in that house."

"Now what?"

"Now we get the money ready for the exchange."

Angrily throwing the cookies down the hall, Bobby slammed the door and bolted each lock to make sure it was secure. Storming off into the kitchen, he rambled through the drawers until he found the sharpest knife he could find. Holding it up in the air to check out the edges, he noticed the blinds were open. With a smug grin, Bobby closed the drawer and walked over to turn the blinds down.

"The only way to freedom is between me and the grave." He mumbled to himself as he crept down the hall. "It's sad, but she forced my hand." Reaching for the handle. "You want to play?" Staring Tami eye to eye as he stood in the doorway with the knife in his left hand. "Then, let's play." Easing the door closed, slowly with his right.

Lost for words, Cameron couldn't believe her eyes. It was as if the place she had always known as her home, had been infiltrated by terrorist. In one week's time. Her lovely, safe, and quiet abode. Had become the center of the combat zone. People were on stake outs, unmarked squad cars were parked down the street, and neighbors were pulling out hand guns on innocent women selling cookies. Things had definitely been taken up a notch. It was only a matter of time before she started seeing hookers standing on the curb and dope dealers selling dope at the bus stop. Something needed to be done and if she had to get involved just to keep the peaceful lakeside view in her backyard. Then, she was fully ready to play inspector snitcher.

"Girl…" Serenading in the receiver as she rushed back to the window to check and see if the coast was clear.

"What is it now, crazy lady?"

"Honestly, you wouldn't believe me if I told you." Standing in the middle of her living room with her left hand on her elbow, right hand on phone, and phone pressed against her ear. Staring blankly into the abyss as she tried to press rewind mentally on what she'd just witnessed.

"I don't believe half the stuff that comes out your mouth anyway, but that's neither here nor there." Shaking her head as she awaited the reporter to announce the headlining news.

"Girl, I just saw Shelly hot tailing it out my neighbor's yard."

"What…"

"Yes, honey." Cameron bragged. "But, you'd never guess why." Flopping down on the couch.

"Why?" Anxious to hear what happened.

"Girl, Bobby pulled a gun out on her and made her hand over the cookies and leave."

"Cookies!" Confused on why Shelly was holding cookies.

"Yeah!" Crossing her legs as she got cozy with one of the pillows. "I guess that was her disguise."

"You think her cover was blown?" Forcing her fingers through her braids to scratch her itching scalp.

"I don't think so." Cameron noted nonchalantly. "I think if her cover was blown. He wouldn't have let her go."

"True."

"I don't know what made him react the way he did. I know whatever it was, really had both of them spooked." Trying to think of reasons why Bobby would feel threatened by a cookie pusher. "It couldn't have been over the price, I know." Ruling out the thought of him robbing her over a three dollar product.

"Na… Something either had to been said or done." Stephanie added.

"I know the other day when I was letting Bear out to relieve himself. Bobby and I got to talking for a bit and I heard a loud bang come from the inside of his house." Wondering if it happened again, and who could have been making the noise. "He took off before I could ask him was everything ok."

"Didn't you say he lived alone?"

"Yeah."

"Do you think he's hiding something?"

"I don't know about all that. But I do know something is going on, especially now that the feds are involved."

"Do you want to come and spend the night with me for a couple of days or at least until things cool down?" Extending an olive branch to offer Cameron a safe haven away from all of the drama.

"Thanks, but no thanks." She refused as she walked back over to her window to see if anyone else was walking up to his door. "I think I'm going to tough it out over here for a while. Just to see what I can dig up on my own." Smiling at the chance to reenact one of her favorite criminal shows. "I want to see what he's hiding and the only way we'll find out is by me staying." Thinking of a way to get herself invited into his home.

"Okay." Shrugging her shoulders effortlessly. "Suit yourself."

SCRIPPER LOVE

Smoke was everywhere from all of the lit cigarettes that were being smoked in such a compact area of the 'Strip'. Wherever you saw a man, a woman wasn't too far behind asking if he needed anything. Reese was sitting at the center table close by the stage. Awaiting the main attraction to come out and perform her solo segment, dipping his cigar in his shot of Hennessy. He slouched down in his seat to make himself more comfortable so he could clear his mind of the encounter he had the other day with Cameron.

"I got to get this chick out my head." He said to himself as he puffed.

While the DJ began fading the current track he was playing out. Reese was releasing the remaining smoke from his nostrils, when he saw her standing in the shadows on the stage.

"Man I love the strippers." He sang as he tapped the ash off his Cuban into the tray compliments of the club.

As the smooth harmonizing sounds of 'I'm in love with a stripper' by 'T-Pain' started to play in the background, the dancer took to the middle of the platform and gave the audience a full view of her center fold. Most of the weekend regulars adored Bam-Bam when it was her turn to brace the stage, because she was known to make her butt clap like it was giving off a

85

round of applause.

Reese wasn't a fan of wasting money on things that he could live without, especially paying for entertainment as such. But, when he needed to unwind and free his mind. He'll come and make it rain. As he sat in front of the stage, Bam-Bam slowly moved her hips in a circular motion to the sounds of 'Cater 2 U' by Destiny Child. She slung her sixteen inch weave and rocked her prop chair back and forth as if to be riding a horse in a seductive manner. Every eyeball in that building was glued on her at that moment. Even her fellow co-workers were jock-ing her skills and were dazzled by the way she massaged herself as a bucket of water fell onto the stage, covering her in a pool of wetness. Bam-Bam was every man's fantasy and every woman's nightmare.

"Damn..." Reese mumbled as he held his drink up against his lips.

Placing the glass back down on the table. He stood up a little to straighten out his boxers, because his erection was trapped between his left leg and the opening. Which had become uncomfortable for him, being he was well endowed and not a mini-man. After taking his seat, Bam-Bam came over and placed her arms around his chest from behind.

"What's your fantasy?" She whispered in his ear.

Intrigued by her choice of words, Reese said nothing in response. But he gave her a playful grin. Asking a man such as himself to tell a woman what his fantasy was, was unorthodox. It wasn't the fantasy that concerned him, it was how willing was the accompanying party willing to participate.

"You're asking too many questions." Pulling her by the hand to direct her in front of where he sat. "Dance." He demanded as he inhaled on the Cuban.

Even though Reese eyes were planted on the ass that seemed to be chewing the hell out of the silk thong Bam-Bam was wearing. His mind was focused on what he said to Cameron the other day. Hurting her feelings wasn't intentional, it kind of just happened. He didn't know what came over him to make him speak to her in such a manner. Maybe he was afraid of opening up and she'd shut him down or something. Or maybe he figured he wasn't good enough.

"Na, that's not the case."

"What's that?" Bam-Bam asked, who was in a full hand stand split.

Realizing he was still sitting in the strip club. Reese got up from his chair and left a tip on the table for the dancer. He didn't say a word to her and he didn't look at her either. He just pulled on one last suck from his cigar and laid it in the ash tray.

Laying in a tub full of bubbles, listening to 'Epiphany' by Chrisette Michele. Stephanie soaked with a calming smile on her face as she enjoyed the warmth of the water. Her fiancé was due home in a couple of hours and she wanted to be ready for his return. Even though Stephanie enjoyed her freedom every now and again. Having too much time alone wasn't good for anybody.

She tried her best to keep herself occupied and with the help of the one and only scandalous Cameron. The time flew by rapidly. Being in the middle of drama was not her cup of tea, but listening to it was more up her alley. With Cameron's new neighbor and Shelly going on stake outs nowadays. She couldn't wait to ease some of the pressure she had built up with Rico.

After having spent about a good hour and a half in the tub. Stephanie finally decided to get out, because the coolness started to disgust her. Using a bathrobe to cover her naked body, she stepped in front of the foggy mirror and smeared her hand across the glass. Reaching over for her tooth paste. She unscrewed the cap and squeezed a nice heap onto her brush.

"Man I need to do better with my daily moisturizing." Examining the dry spots on the sides of her face. "I don't want to look no older than I already am." Spewing the paste out into the vessel sink.

Filling her mouth with a cap filled with scope mouth wash to give her breath that extra freshness she felt would go the extra mile. Stephanie rushed through her last bit of preparations in the restroom and eased in the bedroom.

Because the love birds were going to spend the evening at home, she didn't bother picking out anything to wear. Instead she slid on a tasteful negligee and flipped on the radio. Since Rico had been gone for what seemed like an eternity. Stephanie wanted to remain in the mood for as long as possible. Grabbing her cellular phone from her night stand to browse the internet for some porn. She noticed there were two text messages and four missed calls.

"I must've had that bathroom radio blasting if I've missed these many calls." Punching in her password to unlock the keypad.

Scrolling through the list, she saw majority of the calls came from Rico and one was from Reese. Stephanie figured something had to be wrong if Reese called her personal cell. They were cordial at work and conversed several times regarding their outside life, but it never got to a point to where they called one another at home. Continuing to check her messages. One was from Reese of course, asking her to give him a call. And the other was from her fiancé, stating he was going to be late and advising her not to wait up for him.

"What!" She yelled out in anger, because she felt she put too much effort into preparing for his return. To only receive a notice that she will have to continue to wait to get some love below. "I swear he lucky I love him. Because if it was another chick, she wouldn't be sitting home waiting for him." She grumbled. "I'm tired of staring at these walls every night all night." Rolling out of bed to flip the light switch on. "Let me check and see what Reese wants, before I set it off in this mother fucker."

Riding in circles, Reese was slightly tipsy when he got the call. Before he decided to answer, he thought of what it was exactly he wanted to discuss with Step. He didn't have to many friends he could confide in and talking to his baby mama about another woman was definitely out the question. They were cool, but not that cool.

"Yo…" He greeted while turning the volume nozzle on the dash board down.

"Hey, I got your message. What's going on?" Propping the refrigerator door wide open.

"Nothing really, just heading back to the crib." Avoiding diving straight into what's been ailing him.

Stephanie was a very patient woman. Being she was raised in a house full of men, eight to be exact. She learned to notice the warning signs of a man in pain. Something was wrong, but she wasn't a mind reader. And, she didn't have Mrs. Cleo hanging from her door step either.

"So tell me, what did I do to deserve a home call from you?" Frustrated because her mind was still focused on her fiancé and why the heck he wasn't coming straight home to her.

"Man!" Contemplating on where he should begin. "I got so much on my mind right now and you were the only person I could think of to call." *Damn, he ain't got no homeboys he can confide in.* She thought as she rambled through the cold box.

After having decided on going with the grapes instead of the pineapples, Stephanie reached in her upper cabinet for a bowl to place them in. Nothing was more relaxing then stuffing her face to take her mind off her own selfish dilemmas. After running some cold water over the batch, she welcomed the conversation, because she could really use a little gossip right about now.

"Spill it." She encouraged while chopping down on the juice filled oval.

"See, it's like this." Nervous because he was about to be vulnerable with his manager and he had never been open about his feelings to any woman ever before. "I saw your girl the other day at 'Marcels'."

"I know, she called me after she saw you." Leaning over her counter top, gazing out the window at the stars. Still munching on her delicious midnight treat.

"I kind of figured she would." He snickered.

"You're damn right she did." Appalled by his nonchalant demeanor. "What made you think you could say something like that to her? What type of woman do you take her for? That's my best friend and you know I don't roll like that!"

"I know, but I didn't mean for the conversation to go down the way it did." He admitted. "I was nervous! What you expect?" Shrugging his shoulders. Ashamed as he remembered the look of disgust Cameron had in her eyes.

"Nervous about what!" Halting in mid chew. Still taking her anger out on him because it was really Rico she wanted to be feuding with at that point.

"Because…"

"Because what?" Confused on what could have made Reese nervous about talking with Cam and wanting to get to the bottom of why he hurt her friend.

"Because I like her!" Slamming his left hand down on the stirring wheel. "I like her." Lowering his voice.

"What…" Shocked by the news, yet thrilled. "You don't say." Going straight into match maker mode. "Well, you sure do have a unique way of showing it." She giggled.

"I didn't mean to be brash with her. I just didn't know how to start a conversation with her." Feeling his shoulders tensing up. "Everything started out fine at first," he recalled. "I brought dinner for us both and we started flirting a bit. The next thing I know, I choked up and went in for the kill. And it went downhill from then on."

"The kill!" She blurted out in laughter. "You killed it alright!" She continued to joke. "Murdered it is more like it. Ha, haa.."

"If you're just going to laugh, than forget I ever came to you for your advice."

"Na, na playa…" She said as she wiped her tears. "I'm sorry. I've never heard of a man ruining his opportunity to make a pass on a woman because he got scared. And I've got seven brothers."

"I wasn't scared." Defending his integrity as a man.

"Scared, nervous, they're both the same thing if you ask me."

"Anyway, the reason I called is to see if she was dating anyone and if she wasn't. Could you set something up for me?"

"Well my boy, you're in luck." Placing her bowl in the sink. "I just happen to know she isn't seeing anyone at the moment and she likes you as a matter of fact. That's until you blew it." She chuckled once more.

Heart broken, Reese turned the key in his ignition and gazed in amazement. He couldn't believe Cameron liked him and she'd only seen him at his worse. She didn't deserve the ass he gave her to kiss the other day and he felt horrible about it. If there was a way he could redeem himself, he knew using Stephanie would be the key.

"So, what do you recommend I do to win her over?"

"Give me a couple of days to see what I can cook up. When I get her final opinion about you, I'll give you a call."

"Deal, thanks again Step. I really appreciate it."

"No problem, just don't go hurting nobody else feelings no time soon."

"I won't," he laughed.

Now that Stephanie had straightened everything out with Reese. She needed to get down to the bottom of why Rico wasn't coming home tonight. It wasn't like him to not come to the house when he was in town. Even though, she's been noticing him dragging in a little later than usual lately for his past several returns. Since they were engaged to be married, it never crossed her mind that he'd be out cheating. But, you can't put nothing pass anybody nowadays.

Pouring some dish detergent in the sink, Stephanie went ahead and washed the few dishes she had piled up. Zoned out in the motion, she was distracted by a sudden movement on the counter top where she stood. Glancing slightly to her right, only using her eyes. She saw the roach peeping back at her from underneath the cookie jar. Startled, she eased the dish rag down in the water and leaned to her left to grab the raid.

"DIE BITCH!" Talking to the roach as she sprayed, while the critter attempted to escape. "Whoa!" She yelled, because the determined little guy shot across the counter towards her and leaped. "You got to be kidding me!" Looking around on the floor to see if she could catch him before he got away. Fortunately for the bug, he got a chance to die another day. "I didn't have this roach problem, until Cameron started coming around." Slamming the raid on the table before she left the kitchen. "I'm going to bed."

The freshness of the mid-night breeze, calmed Rico as he drove his F-150 into 'The Ranch' parking lot. Relieved to be off the road for a few days and eager to meet some new people. He had no intention of being cooped up in the house with Stephanie this time around. Even though Rico loved his fiancé dearly. He wanted to dip back in the stable before his commitment became official.

Walking in the front door, Rico instantly felt at home. Crazy alcoholics were cheering on their fellow alki, as she tried her hand at karaoke at center stage. A few ruff necks were having an arm wrestling match, and the rest were mingling and playing poker. Complete freedom and acceptance was in the air. Ready to bask in the ambience, Rico motioned for the bartender to concoct him a Brandy on the rocks. To him, it was nothing wrong with putting a few extra strings on the chest to show how mannish he could be. And a sip of that good ol brown would do the trick.

Tensing up from the smooth flow of his beverage flowing down his throat. Rico was startled when he felt a hand resting on his right shoulder from behind. "Excuse me." A soft spoken voice serenaded in his ear. Unsure if he should be nice or rude. He decided to turn and face her first. Five feet and two inches of pure beauty, stood before his eyes. With a pair of Cowboy boots and a hat to match. Speechless, Rico gazed into her hazel eyes as if to be under hypnosis. "Are you okay?" She asked while waving her hand back and forth across his face. "Hello…." She continued as she snapped her finger.

Rico was mesmerized. Stephanie was pretty. Kind of average. But, never in a million years had he seen a life size, fun size, beauty as the one that stood before him. He tuned out the music and the surrounding chatter as soon as he laid eyes on her. Realizing he was about to miss his opportunity. Rico quickly snapped out of the trance, when he noticed she was turning away.

"Yes." Grabbing her hand to turn her back in his direction. "Yes." Gulping down the rest of the contents in the glass, before he placed it on the napkin.

"Are you okay?" Tucking her Louis clutch under her arm.

"I'm fine, why'd you ask?" Resting his left hand on his hip, while he used the other to wipe the sweat from his forehead. "Do I look ill or something?"

"No…" She chuckled. "You just looked a little lonely and when I spoke it was as if your mind was on another planet." She explained with concern on her face.

"Well, I have a girlfriend. Therefore, I'm not lonely. And it's just, when I first saw you, my breath was taken away by your beauty." Cracking a smile.

The mystery woman smiled at his gesture and ordered herself a 'sex on the beach' to drink. Astonished by her choice, Rico ordered another round of what he was having before she came.

"So, tell me. Is that what you like?"

"What's that?" Twirling her straw around the rim of the glass.

"Sex on the beach." Pulling his pants leg up to loosen the space between his crotch.

"Umm…" She flirted. "I like the fact that you have a girlfriend."

"Ha! Ha!" He choked. "Cold, that's cold." He laughed as he held his glass in hand. "But, you're right. I do." Shaking his head. "So, what brought you over this way?" Referring to her reason for approaching him.

"Entertainment."

"Entertainment?" Failing to understand what she meant by that. Before Rico could ask her to explain. His alarm went off on his cellular phone to let him know it was one o'clock. Even though he had just gotten there. He didn't want to be disrespectful to Stephanie by staying out all night. When he looked up to excuse himself from the conversation. The walking beauty was gone. "Was she an angel?"

Rushing out to the lot, Rico spotted her walking near the valet. Unsure of what he was going to say or what he was doing. He ran over to get her attention. "Why did you leave?" Breathing deeply in an attempt to catch his breath. Having an asthma attack in front of a woman he was trying to impress wasn't on Rico's list of things to do. "I look down to check my phone and when I silenced it. You were gone." Passionate about the way she chose to flee the scene. "I didn't even get a chance to catch your name."

"It's Monique." Rubbing her hands down the sides of her arms to warm them up. "But, my friends call me Mo."

"Well, it was a pleasure meeting you Ms. Mo." Sliding his hands down in his jean pockets. "When can I see you again?"

"I don't know." She blushed. "Ask your girlfriend."

"Ha! Ha! Again with the girlfriend low blows." Shaking his head as he tried to hold back his fascination with her. "It's cool, it's all good." Looking up at her to get a glimpse of her eyes once more. "You have a right to keep throwing it up in our conversation."

"Exactly." Turning to continue to follow the path to her vehicle.

"At least if you ever change your mind. Maybe you could give me a call one day." Handing her a napkin with his telephone number on it.

"One day." Tucking the paper in her purse as she reached in for her keys. "Good night, mister…."

"Rico." Finishing her statement. "It's Rico." Bending down to kiss her hand.

"Ok." She giggled. "Don't get yourself in trouble now."

"Na, na now." Licking his lips seductively. "Don't you go getting yourself in trouble."

"Good night, Rico." She said, giving her last farewells before she pressed her foot on the accelerator.

"Damn." Watching her Maxima drive off in the abyss.

THUG LIFE

Popping out of bed to shut her alarm clock off. Cameron was more determined today than ever before, to get down to the bottom of why her neighbor has been acting so suspicious. Since she had already made up in her mind that she wasn't going to work that morning, she texted her manager the night before, stating she wasn't coming in. Throwing on some sweats and skipping breakfast. Cameron slide on her sun glasses and placed a baseball cap on her head, and slammed the door behind her.

"I need to stop by the hospital and see what else Arnez can tell me about what happened to him the other night." Backing out of her driveway. "How are they connected?" She questioned herself as she viewed her neighbors door step from her rear view mirror.

Before Cameron was clear of her subdivision, she saw a white neon pulling in the gate. Because she placed her phone on silent when she got up, she didn't hear it ring when Dexter was trying to buzz himself in.

"Beep, beep." Honking the horn to catch her attention.

"Good morning!"

"Oh, hey Dexter!" Surprised to see him out and about this early in the day, knowing he'd usually be home babysitting the kids. "What brings you in my neck of the woods today?" She asked. *'Unannounced'*. She mumbled.

"Well, I realized I hadn't heard from the infamous Cameron lately. So, I decided to swing on by since I had been missing you and all." Licking his lips in a flirtatious manner.

"Ha, ha…" She laughed. "Dexter, I'm flattered that you've missed me. Really, but what ever happened to calling first?" Giggling at his sorry attempt to make this visit a booty call. "So, we just pop up on one another now?"

"Nawl, nawl…" Embarrassed by her reaction to him trying to be spontaneous. "I wanted to do something random to keep the spice in our relationship."

"RELATIONSHIP!" Confused by his choice of words. "Sweetie, what we have is an understanding. You have a relationship with the woman you go home to every night. What we have is called 'sex'." Leaning over to check the time on her dash board. "But, I can't do this with you right now." Pressing her foot on the brake to shift her gear back in drive. "I'll call you later on this week." Attempting to blow him off. "I'm kind of in a hurry." Leaving Dexter clueless to what just took place.

After checking in with the receptionist. Cameron walked into Arnez's room for the first time. She wasn't as close to him as Shelly, because they knew each other from meeting at the club. But, she was dear enough to be allowed in his room. Seeing Arnez beat up the way he was lying in bed, made Cameron feel as though she was having hot flashes. She heard he was jacked up, but she never would've guessed it would be this bad. When she stepped in the door, Arnez was gazing out the window so he didn't notice her when she came in. Until, she placed her hands on his arm.

"How are you feeling Super Man?" Rubbing her left hand across his forehead.

"Not so super, but I'm breathing." Adjusting his body in her direction.

"Looks like somebody may need to learn some new moves," she joked. Wanting to lighten up the mood in the room.

"You always know the right time to be an ass." He smiled. "What brings you by my bed side?" Motioning for Lewis to come in and take a seat.

"I heard what happened to you through the grapevine and I wanted to stop in and see if there was anything I could do to help."

"I really appreciate your concern, but we got everything under control now." Covering his muzzled cough. "Let me introduce you to my cousin Lewis." Pointing to Lewis who was standing by the door post. "He works for a secret government tactical team."

When Cameron turned to shake his hand, she couldn't believe the guy that stood before her. Lewis and Cameron went way back to their high school years. They never dated, but word on the halls was he had a crush on her. She never gave him the time of day, because he always had an edge about himself, one that caused her to keep her distance.

The last she ever heard of him, was that he was a dirty cop. But, no one could ever pin any hard evidence on him. And the one person that could, which was his former partner. Got killed in a gun fight they got into on a drug bust. Some say Lewis set him up, because he found out they were paying him off not to sweep the area. But, no one came forward with any solid evidence and the dope dealers wasn't going to rat out no cop.

"Well, well, well... Ms. Cameron Cheeks. It's been a while." Walking in her direction with his arms wide open.

"Lewis McDaniel, long time no see."

"I guess the saying is true."

"What's that?"

"Some people looks never change." Complimenting her as his eyes wondered up her frame.

"I can't say all of that." Using her right hand to assist with flipping her hair to the back. "My hips did spread a bit."

"And it is a blessing." He added.

"Not right now, Lewis." She chuckled with a sarcastic demeanor.

"You're right." He agreed. "I'll get you next time."

"Tell me how you guys know one another again."

"We came out the same year at Astro High." Cameron responded abruptly.

"Oh…" Tucking the covers underneath his leg. "Good, now that we have the formals out the way. We can get down to business. What's the latest?"

"Everything went as planned the other day with the decoy." Lewis begun explaining. "We had a minor bump in the road, but it was smooth sailing after that."

"Did you get the bugs in?"

"Yeah, and we have confirmation that Tami is there and alive as well."

Arnez eyes started to sting as the water flooded his lids. Nothing mattered more to him than to know and hear that his sister was alive. Anything that she may have been going through at that time was only temporary. But, his rescuing her from that sick bastard was guaranteed. Cameron didn't say anything. She just quietly stepped to the side, so she could continue to get an ear in on what was going on. Now that Arnez got the information he needed. The only thing that was left for them to do was to move in and bust her out.

"So, what do we do now?"

"We wait."

"For what!" Furious because he didn't see the need in allowing his sister to remain in bondage any longer than she had to be. "What are you waiting for?" Ready to jump out of bed and go save her himself.

"They asked for a ransom." He stated as he approached the bed. "Therefore, we need a couple of days to pull all of our resources together to pay them."

"If my memory serves me correctly. We don't have a couple of days to come up with $700,000. Them bitch ass niggas want their money today!" Slamming his fist down on the mattress as he grew angrier at the realization that they were running out of time. "Unless you got something worth hearing to tell me. I don't want to hear it."

"We can guarantee an extension if we offer them one million for an immediate release and no one gets hurt."

"A million dollars!" Confused on why his cousin would even suggest that he offer up more money, instead of giving them what they asked for. But, little did he know. Lewis was trying to make good on what he was owed. "How in the hell are we going to come up with that kind of money?" Stressed from concentrating too hard on the specifics. "When we're having a hard time coming up with the seven hundred thousand!"

"Just think about it." Trying to convince Arnez to consider another angle to strategize from. "It's all about manipulating the mind."

"Fuck that shit you're talking about! Are you really trying to play Russian Roulette with Tami's life right now?" Questioning his cousins loyalty.

Cameron couldn't believe it. The strategy Lewis was trying to propose made since, but something about the whole ordeal didn't sit well with her. Here is a chance to get his cousin back alive for $700,000. Which he was already having problems with rounding up. And now, he's trying to risk everything on a hunch. Things couldn't get any weirder then this.

If only I had a beer right now. She mumbled to herself. *This that stuff you see in the movies.*

"No!" Lewis shouted. "I'm just trying to buy us some time, because we don't have the money!"

"You guys just calm down." Finally stepping in to be the medium in the conversation. "I'm pretty sure we all can think of another way, if we just calm ourselves down and work together."

"How do you expect me to be calm, when a nigga got my sister locked up in his house, and this nigga standing in my face asking me for more money that I don't have?" Noticing the alarm going off on the pressure machine he was hooked up to.

"Well, if you don't calm down Arnez. The nurse is going to come in here and kick both us out and wont nothing get resolved." She advised.

"What now, then?"

"Remember, you do have a trust fund your parents left for you and Tami before they died." Bringing up the fact that Arnez had some money saved away.

"I forgot all about that." Remembering he did have a trust, but he never had to use it because he made a way for himself through his own investments.

"It only takes two business days for the bank to clear your signature and release it to your personal account."

How do he know all of that... Cameron thought.

"But by it being a large amount. They may do it by increments. Or, you can opt to get it in full. They will issue you a check, but you'll have to go to a branch to sign off for it first."

"Let's do it." Arnez agreed without further hesitation.

"Deal, I'll get the papers started as soon as I leave." Lewis said as he pulled the blanket over Arnez's shoulders to tuck him in.

"I'll see you later Arnez. I have a few errands I need to run before I head home."

"Alright then Cam." Giving her a nod of approval. "Thanks again for stopping by."

"Don't mention it." Kissing him on the forehead.

No one knew what Lewis had stuffed up his sleeve. Even though, he loved his cousin dearly. He still haven't gotten over the fact that she ripped him off a few years back. When she asked him to get in on a heist she had planned against one of her regular customers.

"Yo…"

"Hey Lewis." Tami greeted.

"What's good fam?" Parked on the side of Metropolitan parkway, waiting for speeders.

"I need a huge favor and you know I got you on the share of the loot." Whispering out of paranoia.

"What's going on?" Suddenly vested in the opportunity to make some fast cash.

"Listen, I have some up state dudes coming in around midnight tonight to pick up a few keys from me. And, they're going to be carrying a hefty fifty g's." She explained. "All I need for you to do is, show up to the drop off location. But keep your distance and use your bull horn to announce you have us surrounded." Feeding him the rundown of the plan. "Once you say that." Pausing to make sure no one was listening in on her conversation. "I'm going to snatch the brief case and drive off." She smiled. "The only thing left for you to do, is pull up." Checking behind all the doors in the restroom. "Don't chase them though, because they will be armed. And, they're willing to shoot if you pursue." Making sure he stuck to the plan down to the tee. It was one thing to ask her cousin to risk his job for some cash, but, risking his life wasn't an option.

"It sounds like you've thought this thing all the way through."

Impressed by his little cousins ability to think like a man.

"Yeah, I'm done with these outside connects. They trying to raise the ticket price, because the gas prices been going up." Pissed at the thought of paying taxes on drugs. "And, I can't fuck with that."

Tami got her supply from an out of state dealer, but she sold to up state dealers as well. Ever since the economy plummeted. The people she had been buying from upped their charge, because of fueling prices to gas up the boat that transported the merchandise to the U.S..

"What's in it for me? Numbers to be exact?" Debating whether or not her offer will be worth the risk.

"Half."

"That's fair." Watching two teens jay walk across the intersection, instead of using the cross walk. "Count me in."

"I'll call you at eleven thirty to give you the location." She advised before she hung up the telephone.

It was eleven fifteen when Lewis got the call. She let him know they were meeting in the plaza on Buford Highway and he should post up on the side of the Burger Bean. Everything went as planned down to the snatch and run, to the fake FBI bust. Lewis adrenaline was racing through his body. The thrill of the high excited him and he was ready to reap his reward. But, when he called Tami to see where she was going to meet him. Her number was disconnected. How ironic he thought. Furious that he may have just gotten played by his own flesh and blood. He did a quick drive by her house, when he saw a note she had left for him on the door. "Dear Lewis: April fools." It read. The house was abandoned and he had no way of contacting her.

You see, Tami was smarter than he expected. She knew if she stiffed him. There was nothing he could do about it. He couldn't file a report.

What would it say? I went on an unauthorized drug bust by myself and the criminals got away. He couldn't say he got robbed of twenty five thousand dollars, because the agency would do an investigation on him regarding how he got that kind of doe instantaneously and question its legitimacy. Lastly, he couldn't report it. Because it was all caught on camera. The whole exchange, the fake bust, and the moment he didn't pursue the suspect and shut off his sirens. Was all caught on candid camera.

Tami played Lewis all the way around in a 360 degrees trap. She never intended on splitting the money with him from the beginning, when she chose Buford Highway as the meet spot. She knew there were cameras all around that strip and that's how she knew she had the perfect scheme. Tami wasn't new to this, she was true to this. And if you didn't have the heart for the life style she lived. You couldn't make it in the street game of life.

"And Lewis."

"Yeah…" Turning back to face Arnez.

"Make them bastards pay."

"Most definitely."

Shelly had been shook up since the incident that happened with Bobby on her stake out the other day. She knew Arnez didn't intentionally put her in a compromising position on purpose. But, she couldn't say the same about his cousin. The way he reacted to her when she was having her panic attack, was very insensitive of him. And if she didn't know any better. She felt he would have let Bobby kill her if it meant saving his evidence without blowing his case.

"Police can be so unhuman sometimes." She said to her eighteen month old son, who was stacking up his alphabet blocks. "I can't even begin to imagine not being able to come home to you and those dimples every day." Sitting on the floor in Indian style in front of him. "My heart hurts now just thinking about that almost being our reality yesterday." Watching her love child play innocently with excitement. "I love you Lamar." She cried.

"Is everything alright in there?" Michael asked. Walking in and placing his keys on the banister.

"Yeah, I'm fine." She lied. "I was just thinking about what happened the other day." Wiping the tears from her eyes. "That's the second time my life was almost snatched away from me over some b.s.."

"I know what you mean."

"Do you!" She argued. "Or are you just saying that to make light of the situation?" Finally breaking down the tough barrier she built emotionally and allowed the tears to flow.

"Shelly, I would never do or say anything to make you feel that I'm not being genuine with you." Kneeling down on his knees to wrap his arms around her. "I love you, hot stuff."

"I know poo bear, but I can't understand why this stuff keeps happening to me." Embracing him back. "I've done nothing to deserve what's been happening to me."

"I know, I know." Using his hands to wipe her tears away. "Maybe God is trying to warn you or something."

"Warn me about what?" Confused by his statement.

"I don't know. That's something you need to go to him and discuss."

"But, when do I have time?" Putting pressure on the sofa to help herself up. "I'm always at the shop and when I come home. I have to see about Lamar and cook dinner. Once I get everything situated, it's time to do it all over again."

"There's your problem right there."

"What?"

"You have to take the initiative to make time." Picking Lamar up from the floor.

"Maaa, ma." He chanted as he reached his little pudgy hands out for her.

"If you can manage us and still have time to exercise. I know you can fit at least five minutes in to talk to the man up above." Carrying the baby off with him into the kitchen. "Life is what you make it!" He shouted. "We all have choices!"

After soaking in what the love of her life just counseled her on, Shelly received a text. *I wonder who this is.* She thought to herself as she reached in her pocket. *Maybe it's Niko checking in on me. I know I haven't talked to her in a while. She may be texting to tell me she got that job.* **Unknown number: I want to see my daughter....**

"What was that?" Michael asked Lamar after he placed him in his play pin. "Shelly!" He yelled after hearing a loud bang. "Is everything alright in there?" Coming out of the baby's room to see where that noise came from. "I heard something hit the floor and I wanted to know if you heard it to." Walking back into the living room. "SHELL!!!"

LIFE'S A WITCH

Gazing off into space. Bobby sat in his rocking chair and let the fire on his cigarette burn down to ashes, as he stared off into the deep blue sky. Where did he go wrong? When did he allow things to get out of his control? When he took Tami, it was never his intention to do any physical harm to her. He just wanted to spook her up a bit and mess with her mentally. Just to teach her a lesson she would never forget. It never dawned on him that his best friend of all people out of his crew. Would or could be so vindictive. But, to beat up her brother for some ransom money. When there's other ways he could've chose to be petty, put the icing on the cake. Now that they've requested payment for her return. It wouldn't be long before the authorities got involved and Bobby didn't want to be in the mix when that took place.

Coincidentally, the atmosphere was calming for a Monday morning. The peace before the storm as the older generation would call it. The birds weren't chirping and the squirrels weren't flirting. None of the neighbors were out in their yards, and not one car passed by in the past several hours. None of these things didn't come to Bobby's attention, until he looked over and noticed Cameron's car wasn't parked in her driveway. And since he's been living in the neighborhood, Cameron has always made it her business to try to be in his business. Unbeknownst to him; the FBI had the entire parameter blocked off for a few blocks and they were positioning themselves to move in for the take down. Cameron was warned by Lewis not to go home after she left the hospital that morning, because the team would be setting up camp in the area. And they didn't want any unexpected casualties in the mix of the possible gun fire.

While Bobby continued to uneasily sit on his front porch. A white suburban pulled up alongside his mail box. *Speaking of the devil.* He thought to himself as he flicked the bud in the grass. He watched the unit he affiliated himself with, climb out of the truck one by one from a far. When did he become blind to the snakes in his circle? Maybe he accepted them a long time ago when they first met. They say birds of a feather flop together, but in Bobby's case. It was definitely loyalty over reality. Because, in reality. They were all bums. But, because of his ride or die mentality. He's realizing it may cost him more than what he's willing to risk by remaining loyal to his so called friends.

"We need to talk." Paul stated as he brushed pass Bobby and proceeded to walk in the house.

"What's good?" Turk greeted as he followed.

"And good morning to you all as well." Fastening the screen door behind himself. "Have you heard anything from ol' dude yet?"

"Not yet." Paul replied using an irritated tone. "I thought dude would have jumped to rush and deliver the doe, knowing we had his sister."

"I thought he would too." Murf added.

"Hey, hey!" Turning up the volume on his head phones. "We got some action going on in there!" Every officer that were either in decoy vehicles or staked out behind some of mother nature's living decorations. Were all tuned into 'Operation Set it Off', awaiting the signal to move in.

The officers that were on team 'Set it Off', wasn't regular field agents.

They weren't even considered to be pencil pushers or rookies. They were the action craved junkies that the Captain would send out on certain missions, when he didn't care if any of the suspects were brought in dead or alive.

"So…" Breaking the silence in the room. "What are we going to do now that we ain't got no money?" Wanting to let Tami go and head for the border, while they still had a chance to get away scott free.

"Ain't nobody going nowhere!" Paul shouted as he slammed his fist down on the counter top. "Let me clear that thought out of all y'all bitch ass niggas minds right now, before you even get a chance to attempt to think it." Commanding the room. "We're all about to sit in this fucking living room and come up with a new plan of action. To get us out of this mess."

Since none of the guys received any news from Arnez regarding the money. They automatically assumed, he went to the police. Everyone had priors and Paul has a bench warrant out for his arrest at the moment for back child support. Tami could hear all of the commotion coming through the walls from the front room. She had since given up her fight to escape, because all of her other attempts had fell. The only thing she prayed for nowadays, is for her survival. After this big traumatic experience, she promised herself if she got free. She'd let the dope game go.

"Where's that pretty, little, nosey neighbor of yours?" Turk asked as he peered out of the living room window.

"I don't know." Getting more suspicious of her not returning home just yet. "She hasn't been there all morning."

"Maybe she got a man or something."

"I doubt that." Bobby disagreed. "I mean, I see a couple dudes come and go, here and there. But, nothing serious." Grabbing his phone out of his pocket to reference the time. "If she had someone, I'd know about it."

"I heard she was down at the hospital visiting o'l dude." Murf butted in.

"What!" Paul shouted as he stood to his feet. "She know dude?"

"Yeah, I thought y'all knew." Shrugging his shoulders like it wasn't a big deal.

"And you didn't think to tell us this earlier because?" His brother questioned.

"Don't you think if we knew she knew him. We would've took care of her as well." Nervous because Cameron could be the loose end that could get them all locked up. Especially when they've been trying so hard not to have any.

"Yeah, I use to see her talking to him occasionally at that club he owns."

"Fuck!" Paul shouted as he pushed the bar stool down on the floor. Which caused Tami to fear from the loud bang it made. "Am I the only one in this freaking room that's been using his brain through this whole pile of b.s.?" Reaching over the counter to grab a cigarette from his pack.

"Has anybody noticed there ain't been no movement on this street since we got here?"

"I noticed that when I was out sitting on the porch before you guys arrived." Bobby agreed with Turk, who was still peering out the front window.

"What you mean?" Murf asked as he walked over to take a look for himself.

"I mean, I ain't heard or seen no car since we got here and as a matter of fact. I didn't see any when we pulled in the neighborhood either and it's almost 4p.m.."

"Shit!"

"What?" Bobby asked.

"Shh…" Paul instructed as he placed his fingers over his lips to get all the fellas to stop talking.

Picking up a magazine off the coffee table and pulling a pen from the drawer in the kitchen. Paul penciled out everything he needed to say to the fellas, because he suspected some foul shit was about to take place. In the note, he told the twins on the count of four, using his finger of course. They were going to walk out to the truck and leave, and Bobby was to lock up and start packing his things. Only the basic's would do. And to rendezvous with them at the dock around 10p.m. sharp. If he wasn't there by 10:03p.m., they would have to leave without him, because it meant he got caught.

From that moment on they were instructed to only communicate through text. But no one should text anything, because everything that needed to be discussed had been done on that paper. Once the instructions were given, Paul held up his left hand and counted down the seconds and then they took action. Because the agents were cut out of the conversation, they were surprised to see the fellas existing the house and getting in the truck. Confused on what they've missed. They decided to stay neutral, until they figured out what went wrong and what the next move should be.

Rushing in his bedroom, Bobby grabbed his suit case and stuffed a few boxers, t-shirts, jeans, socks, and the last of his stash down in the bag. He figured whatever he missed he'd buy on the road. Spooking Tami as he practically kicked the door off the hinges of the room he had her in. Bobby walked over to her and kneeled on his knees in front of her. She didn't know what to think as this man who'd been torturing her for days, stared at her with fear in his eyes and sweat dripping down the sides of his temple.

"I just want you to know, I never intended on killing you." Using his right hand to push her hair back out of her face.

Tami went into a frenzy, because she knew this was the end. She could sense it in his tone. The least he could've done was given her one last courtesy meal, before she departed from this cruel world.

"All I wanted to do was get revenge on the person that did this to my sister." Laying his head in her lap.

Tami's eyes widened when she realized this was all happening to her because of what she did to Monique. *That damn Monique*, she thought.

"Fuck that thieving bitch!" She shouted under the tape as tears came pouring down her cheeks.

"But, because you had mercy on her and let her live. I'm going to do the same for you." He informed her, looking up into her beautiful dark brown eyes. "Hmmm…" He mumbled. "I wonder how you'd look with green eyes?" Tilting his head slightly to the right. "Anyway, I really wish we could have met under different circumstances. I believe I could have possibly fell in love with you and made you my wife." Running his hand up her leg.

Tami could have burst from all the anguish she was experiencing as he kneeled in front of her, giving a heart to heart.

"But, when life throws you a curve ball. You have to throw that bitch one back." Now standing to his feet. "I really hope you enjoyed my company as I yours." Taking one last look at her. "We could've been something special." Kissing her on the opposite side of the duct tape that was stuck to her lips. "Don't look sad." He advised. "Somebody will find you sooner or later." He chuckled as he turned the light out and shut the door.

Before Bobby could leave, he had to place the letter in Cameron's mailbox that he took his time to write for her. So she could get it when she finally gets home.

"Boss the suspect is on the move." One of the agents radioed Lewis as he sat beside a bush near Bobby's house.

"What he doing?" Curious of what Bobby could have been planning at that moment.

"Right now, he's putting something in the young lady mailbox that stays next door to him."

"Which one?"

"The one to our left."

"Shit!" Lewis shouted. "That's Cameron's mailbox."

"Would you like for us to retrieve the package for you when he heads back in the house?" Awaiting on his orders.

"No." Lewis exhales. "Just leave it in there for now." He instructed. "We'll let her read it first."

"Boss!"

"Yeah…"

"He's coming back out the house with a suit case in tow."

"Cut him off at the first red light."

"Ten four."

Bobby looked down at his watch and it was the moment of truth. It was 9:27p.m. and although it would only take fifteen minutes to get to the dock, give or take an extra five minutes. He didn't want to miss his chariot. Throwing his vehicle in reverse, Bobby anxiously backed out of his driveway with gas on his mind. Because he was so anxious, he decided not to listen to any music, because he didn't want anything to distract him from remaining focus.

While he exited the gated neighborhood, he noticed he still hadn't seen no sign of life since he left his door step.

"Something ain't right." Pressing his foot on the brake as he neared the four way traffic light. "Should I run the light or should I wait…" Contemplating back and forth with his thoughts, whether or not to live his life on the edge or remain predictable.

Before Bobby had a chance to decide, he saw flashing lights coming on all sides of his vehicle. He didn't know what to do or think. Behind him, were swat cars. To the left and the right of him, were swat cars. But, straight ahead was a chance to risk it all. As he sat there thoughtless as he watched his life flash before his eyes. Bobby did what any guy would do in his situation and smashed on the gas.

TRUST NO ONE

Because Lewis had advised Cameron not to go home that day, she figured she'd pay Stephanie a visit at 'Lashay's', since she didn't have anything else to do. When she got there, Stephanie was sitting in the lobby eating her lunch, looking as if she had seen a ghost.

"Just one of those days, huh?" She asked as she flopped her 158 pound frame in the booth.

"You don't even know the half."

"Well, I got time." Grabbing one of her fries off her tray.

"Do you know that inconsiderate wangsta didn't come home the other night."

"Naw girl! Say what..." Halting in mid chew.

"Yes!" Slamming her fist down in the table. "He had the nerve to tell me he wanted to hangout that night and get a breather."

"No he didn't!" Shaking her head.

"Oh, yes he did." Filling Cameron in on the latest juice.

"So, what happened? Did y'all get into a fight or something?"

"Nope, not this time around." Resting her head on her hand.

"He just came home the next morning as if nothing happened and went to sleep."

"Did he at least give you a hug or something?" Bring a gift home, or something?" Questioning in a mono tone.

"Yea, he did alright."

"What was it?" Anxious to see what he brought for her.

"Another woman."

"What!" Grabbing her chest as if to stop her heart from popping out of her body.

"Yeah…" Sucking her teeth. "I saw a new number in his contacts and it was a woman name."

"Girl, stop it I say!" Laughing at her friends foolishness. "You doing all this conclusion jumping and this woman can be somebody which is nobody."

"I hope you're right about this Cameron."

"Ain't I always?"

"True." Agreeing with her friend despite her gut insecurities.

"You're just getting cold feet, because the wedding is right around the corner. Everything is fine." She reassures her. "Chill out."

"Alright, I will." Smiling in relief. "Oh, and somebody got an admirer." Perking up from her gloomy state.

"Who?"

"You."

"Who?"

"Him." Pointing at Reese, who was straightening out his area with his headphones in his ear.

"Child please…" Brushing her remark off nonchalantly. "He screwed up his chance."

"Oh, really?"

"Yes, really."

"Does he know that?"

"I don't know, but what does it matter?"

"Well, here's your opportunity to let him know then." Getting up from her seat when she saw Reese approaching.

Cameron didn't know what to do when he sat down in front of her with a smile that could brighten the darkest corner of the earth. In the beginning she found Reese attractive and wanted to get to know him and see if they could possibly build something together. But, after the encounter she had with him a few weeks ago in that restaurant. She thought he was a jerk and didn't deserve a chance to get to know her.

"How's it going?" He asked. Excited to see her face again. But to his surprise, Cameron didn't utter not one word to him. She just stared. "I know we started out on the wrong foot."

"No, you started off with the wrong foot." Cutting him off, before he could complete his statement. "Honestly, if you didn't come over here to apologize to me. Then, there's no need for you to waist anymore of our time." She snapped. Extending the invitation for him to remove himself from the situation.

"If it's an apology you want. Then, I apologize for the way I acted the other day at dinner." Pulling his ear buds from his ear. "I didn't mean to be an ass, it kind of just happened." He sympathized. "I had my guard up, because I didn't know what you were trying to pull with me."

"Pull with you!" She shouted. "If I can recall correctly. I didn't approach or even attempt to make a move on you. That was all you! I came to eat!"

"I feel what you're saying but…"

"But, what?" Cutting him off again. "Had I known you were even there, I would've went somewhere else that night."

"So, it's like that?"

"Yeah, straight like that."

"Say no more." Grabbing his things and walking away from the table.

"Stephanie!" Cameron shouted. "I'm about to go!"

"What happened?" She asked as she scribbled on her chart.

"I'll discuss it with you later, but right now I need to head to the house. I have a puppy I need to attend to."

"Alright then girl. I understand. Just call me later on to let me know you made it there safely."

"I will." Letting the door slam behind her.

During her drive home. Cameron was furious with Reese and how he tried to converse with her as if nothing ever happened. He embarrassed her the other day and have the audacity to come smiling in her face as if everything was all good. And had the nerve to give her that half ass apology as if he meant it. Not today and not with her. Cameron was not a force to be reckoned with.

When she got home, she checked her mail, because she hadn't been there all day. And then, she let Bear out to play for a bit. Even though it was dark out, she knew he was safe. So, she started her bath and opened her first piece of mail that just had her name on it. ***To: Cameron.***

"I wonder who sent this." She said to herself as she slid her finger through the crack in the back. "It doesn't have a stamp or a return address." She blurted out of curiosity. "Maybe someone placed it in after they stopped by and saw I wasn't home." Pulling the note out of the envelope. "Let me see. What do we have here…"

Dear Cameron, I'm going to get you. It read. Immediately after seeing the letter, Cameron tossed it on the counter and went outside to call for her pup. Once she had him in tow, she bolted all of her doors and checked all of her windows to make sure they were secure. Cameron had never been afraid of living alone up until the moment she read the line *'signed, your next door neighbor'*. People sent threatening messages to people all the time. But, it never bothered her. Because she had that security that they would never show up or the peace that they didn't know where she lived. But, the fact that the threat came from less than twenty steps away. The unsettling feeling she had in her gut, couldn't compare to the fear she had in her heart.

TO BE CONTINUED...

ABOUT THE AUTHOR

Born and raised in Atlanta, Georgia. Danielle Walker has always strived to become an entrepreneur since the early age of eight. It started with odd jobs around the house, which soon led to braiding hair for extra cash. Becoming a Corporate Lawyer has always been a dream of hers, but it soon changed in her early semesters of college. Where she had the opportunity to intern for one of Atlanta's most prestigious law firms 'The Mosby Law Group'.

Seeing and experiencing first-hand the hectic-ness of running a law firm. Danielle decided that particular career field wasn't for her. Continuing to work two jobs and maintain being a full-time student. Danielle eventually realized working extremely hard wasn't something she wanted to do either. Later she found herself at a crossroad because she didn't have a plan B.

With life experiences having their way with her and her motivation to make something of herself at its peak. Danielle picked up her pen and did what she felt came natural to her. Today Ms. Walker is the owner of 'YJLM Publishing House' and is the author of one of the best-selling books of 2014. Optimistic for the future, you can guarantee she is ready to take on her next challenge in life one day at a time.

QUESTIONS

1.   What did you expect from the book when you first read the title?

2.   What did you make of Cameron? Did you think she was being to nosey or did you feel she had a right to be suspicious of the guy that moved next to her?

3.   Did you think Bobby was wrong for wanting to seek revenge on the person that took his sister?

4.   Were you surprised when you read what happened to Arnez?

5.   Which of the fellas do you like the most?

6.   What do you think will happen next for Shelly?

7.   Did Lewis catch you by surprise or could you tell from the beginning his character would turn out that way?

8.   Did the ending catch you by surprise?

9.   How did you feel when Bobby started catching feelings for Tami?

10.   Would you read this book again?

CONTACTING THE AUTHOR

You can follow Danielle Walker on social media at her links below:

1. www.4realdanielle.com

2. Dannie_babie@twitter.com

3. Danniebabie07@instagram.com

4. DanielleWalker@Facebook.com

Also be sure to follow:

1. Jdromusic@twitter.com

2. BFlatTrax@twitter.com

3. KD205@twitter.com

4. Hollowent@twitter.com

www.ingramcontent.com/pod-product-compliance
Lightning Source LLC
Chambersburg PA
CBHW050759250626
47155CB00005B/2139